OSLG

HOUSE OF FEAR

Jill's twenty-first birthday is more than just a milestone — it marks the day her life changes forever . . . A letter arrives on the morning of her birthday; an invitation to travel to Crag House on the remote Scottish island of Inver to stay with the grandfather whose existence she had been completely unaware of. Whilst there, she meets her cousins, Owen and George, and handsome neighbour Robert Cameron. But her visit has involved her in a web of deceit that may threaten her life . . .

PHYLLIS MALLETT

HOUSE OF FEAR

Complete and Unabridged

LINFORD
Leicester

First published in Great Britain in 1996

First Linford Edition
published 2013

A catalogue record for this book is available
from the British Library.

ISBN 978–1–4448–1685–3

Published by
F. A. Thorpe (Publishing)
Anstey, Leicestershire

Set by Words & Graphics Ltd.
Anstey, Leicestershire
Printed and bound in Great Britain by
T. J. International Ltd., Padstow, Cornwall

This book is printed on acid-free paper

1

Today was Jill's twenty-first birthday and as she woke up that morning, she hoped the day would be different. On her way downstairs to make breakfast, she paused and tapped at her father's bedroom door.

He had an early appointment with a literary agent, and she mentally crossed her fingers for him as she continued down the stairs, her brown eyes glistening at the sight of four letters on the doormat in the hall.

Inspecting the letters, she discovered that one was addressed to her, a birthday card, judging by the size of the envelope. Two others were obviously bills, and the fourth, a thick, good-quality, white envelope was postmarked Edinburgh. Going into the kitchen, she dropped the letters on the table and got on with breakfast, a job that had been hers for as long as she could remember.

Her father's feet sounded on the stairs as she poured tea into two cups. Jill turned with a ready smile as he entered the kitchen, his greying hair tousled, his eyes puffy from the lack of sleep.

'Happy birthday, darling!' he exclaimed, kissing her cheek. 'I can't believe that you're twenty-one already!'

'And I can't believe you're up and dressed before seven-thirty!'

'It's a big day.' His honest blue eyes still had a youthful spark about them. Then he noticed the letters on the table. 'I hope your birthday card arrived! I'm afraid I posted it a bit late.'

'It arrived this morning. Thanks, Dad!' Jill buttered the toast and put it on a plate for him. 'Yours is the only birthday card I ever get!' A tinge of sadness edged her tone. 'I'll open it in a moment.'

'And the rest are bills!' Jim Telford picked up the letters and scanned them. 'Hello, what's this?' He gazed at the long, white envelope. 'Edinburgh! From Irvine and Bruce, the solicitors!'

'What's so special about a letter from Scotland?' Jill glanced at him. 'And who do you know north of the border?'

'Your mother was Scottish for a start!'

Jim Telford's voice sounded so abrupt that Jill glanced quickly at him. His face was set in unusually harsh lines, which suddenly aged him. Jill frowned, trying to recall all she knew about her mother, who had died giving birth to her.

'I'm sorry, I didn't realise it would upset you, but I don't really know anything else about her,' she said slowly.

'You know it's too painful to talk about that part of my life.' He sat down at the table. 'But I don't think this is mere coincidence! A letter arrives from Scotland on the same day as your twenty-first!'

'Why don't you open it?'

'I can't do that.' He smiled faintly. 'It's addressed to you.'

3

'Me!' Jill gasped. 'Why would a Scottish solicitor write to me?'

'Here's your chance to find out!' His face was impassive but his eyes were gleaming, obviously keen to find out what news his daughter had received.

Jill picked up the letter and turned it over, somehow knowing that the information it contained would have some kind of effect on her life. Letters from solicitors rarely did anything else.

'Well?' her father demanded as moments fleeted silently by.

'It's from a Robert Irvine,' she said, ripping open the envelope and unfolding the letter inside.

'What does it say?'

'My grandfather, Hamish Campbell, wants me to visit him at Crag House on the Isle of Inver.' Jill's throat constricted as she read through the words, her voice becoming a strangled whisper as she re-read the terse communication.

'I didn't even know I had a living grandfather!' She looked up to meet her father's intent gaze. 'I was under the impression that we had no relatives in the world.'

'Your mother's family has never wanted anything to do with us!' A trace of bitterness edged his voice. 'Hamish Campbell must be at least eighty now, but twenty-five years ago, when I first met your mother, he was a tyrant to his two daughters, who were his only family. When your mother died, I didn't keep up with them. I have no idea what became of her sister, Fiona — whether she married or not.

'She and Hamish hated me for what I was. They evidently had far better plans for your mother.' His voice had hardened and his eyes were narrowed at what were obviously bitter recollections. 'And they were probably right!' he added. 'If your mother hadn't married me she might still be alive!'

'Don't say that!' Jill went to his side and put a hand on his shoulder. 'You know how much Mother loved you! You used to tell me all the time how perfectly suited you were!'

'And her death was the end of the world for me.' He nodded gravely. 'If you hadn't survived I would have had nothing to live for. As it was, your mother left me with the responsibility of bringing you up, and while I have you, Jill, I still have a part of her.'

Jill smiled, but she could feel tears welling up in her eyes. She grasped his hand and kissed it, and he looked up at her.

'I suppose I shouldn't have blamed your grandfather for his attitude,' he said softly. 'He didn't like me because I was a struggling writer, and because I wasn't Scottish I couldn't be seen as a suitable husband for your mother.'

'Dad!' Jill pressed a sympathetic hand upon his shoulder. 'That must have been terrible for you!'

He sighed.

'I was prepared to concede to family pressure for your mother's sake, but she didn't want anyone else! We were perfect together! Finally we eloped, and Hamish Campbell cut all family ties!

'She never saw him again, and didn't hear from her sister. When your mother died, I told Hamish, but he never acknowledged the loss, and I only ever received one letter from Fiona.

'That was the last contact I had with them until Mrs Seward, the house-keeper at Crag House, wrote some six years ago, informing me that Fiona had died. Mrs Seward was always on our side. But apart from that I pushed all thoughts of that family out of mind.

'But I've often wondered what will happen when Hamish dies because he owns a large estate in Scotland!' He shook his head, his gaze thoughtful. 'And now you're twenty-one and Hamish wants to see you!'

'Well, I don't want to see him!' Jill spoke firmly.

Jim Telford smiled.

'You have no quarrel with your grandfather, and you do have certain rights. Your mother would want you to go to Crag House, Jill. Despite everything, Hamish Campbell was her

7

father, and your mother loved him deeply.' He paused to gauge the strength of her mood. 'I'm quite sure the right thing for you to do is visit your grandfather.'

Jill caught her breath in a sigh as she gazed at his set face. Quite suddenly her normal, uncomplicated life was in turmoil, and all because of this strange letter which had arrived so abruptly! But she couldn't even consider a decision at this moment, and shook her head slowly.

'I shall need to think about it,' she decided.

'Of course. But just remember that Crag House was your mother's birthplace. If only because of that you should consider your decision carefully. I think you deserve everything your mother didn't have, so remember, if you go, it will be for your mother's inheritance.'

Jill felt torn. She didn't agree with the way her mother and father had been treated but this was a chance to meet her maternal grandfather! She sighed heavily having come to a decision.

'I know what you're saying makes sense and I think I would like to go,' she said slowly.

'Well, you're taking your annual holiday in a month, so reply to this letter, suggesting you make the trip in the first week of June.'

'Let me think it over until this evening,' Jill hedged. She was suddenly filled with a strange, indefinable longing, and felt strangely choked with emotion. 'I need a bit more time.'

Her father nodded.

'I won't attempt to influence you in any way because you must make up your own mind about this. But your grandfather is very old now, and we don't know the state of his health. I suspect that you are heir to the estate, so perhaps Hamish is preparing to settle his affairs. And unless Aunt Fiona had any family, you have a birthright in Scotland.'

Jill nodded and they settled down to

breakfast. But her thoughts were racing and she felt very excited. By the time her father was ready to leave for the city she was very keen to make the visit to Scotland, but resolutely fought down her impatience.

'See you later,' she said at the front door as he departed. 'I hope this agent is kind to you. Best of luck!'

'Thanks, but I'm too old to get excited over prospects!' He reached forward as she craned to kiss his cheek.

'I'll print out the first draft of your new book,' she promised. 'It'll be ready for you when you get back.'

* * *

Jill was thoughtful as she started working. Excitement had unravelled in her mind at the arrival of the letter from Scotland, and in a way she was looking forward to some changes in her life. Not that she could complain about the way it was just now — but she had been in the same routine for years.

She loved working for her father but sometimes the monotony was a little heavy. She had only ever had one small romance in her life, and she stifled a sigh at the recollection. Adrian Miller was the only man who had fired her imagination and stirred her emotions, but he emigrated to Australia with his family two years ago and they had lost contact . . .

By the time she was involved in her work, Jill's thoughts were coloured by the hopes that had taken root in her mind. Her imagination was working overtime, and she was assailed by a host of unrealistic thoughts that flared up like a forest fire despite her determined efforts to keep them under control.

She tried to suppress her excitement, feeling that wanting to see her mother's family was tantamount to being a traitor to her father. But by the end of the day she realised that her mind seemed to have made some decisions of its own. She was now eager to go to Scotland to see her mother's birthplace.

After dinner that evening she re-read the letter from Edinburgh, almost devouring the terse message it contained. It gave only the barest information, and she read it repeatedly, trying to glean more from between the lines.

Then she drafted a reply, accepting the invitation and stating her position. She was taking her annual holiday in June and could spend three weeks at Crag House.

It was quite late when her father returned, and he apologised, aware that she needed to discuss the letter with him, but Jill assured him that she had made her decision without too many problems.

'So you've accepted!' He nodded, his blue eyes bright as he regarded her. 'I'm glad! It's about time something worthwhile happened in your life. I know you're quite content to be here with me but I wouldn't say it's the most exciting life for a girl of twenty-one. Perhaps if your mother had been here things would have been different — but I really think it's time you got out and saw something of the outside world.'

'But, Dad, I wouldn't have had my life any other way!' Jill said loyally. 'I'm quite happy with the way my life has turned out! You haven't failed me in any way. You've given me a good home and always looked after me. I couldn't have wanted more!'

'But now it's time for you to go it alone,' he mused. 'I've brought you up and hopefully given you a good grounding. Now it is up to your grandfather. But I shall miss you, Jill. You've been my life from the day you were born.'

'Miss me!' She frowned. 'But I'm only going for three weeks! It's no different from any other holiday I've taken!'

'But this is different!' He smiled sadly. 'I have this feeling that once you're there you won't be coming back!'

Jill was shocked by his words.

'What do you mean? Of course I'll

come back! This is my home, and I want to be with you. Why should you think I won't be coming back?'

'Because that's how it'll be if you inherit your grandfather's estate! You will have to stay there. I telephoned Robert Irvine this morning and gleaned more information. As I told you, there was just your mother and her sister, Fiona. Well, Fiona married a man who had two sons by a previous marriage, but she never had children of her own.

'So you're Hamish Campbell's only blood relation, and a will in your favour has been in existence since your Aunt Fiona died. The entire estate is left to you, and Hamish has no intention of changing that will. And that's why he wants to see you before he dies!'

'I can't believe it!' She shook her head dazedly. 'It's all happening so quickly!'

'But it is happening nevertheless!' Her father smiled, his eyes bright. 'I'm very happy for you. But things will be a lot different from now on.'

Jill had a vision of her world falling to pieces, because of all these changes! And she didn't want to be apart from her father! This way of life was all she had ever known, and anything else was too frightening to cope with.

'But why should I leave here altogether?' she said tentatively.

'Because the will says so.' He nodded emphatically. 'There's a clause to be considered. If you don't live at Crag House, at least until the death of Hamish Campbell, then the estate will be shared between the two stepsons Fiona brought up.'

'Oh!' Jill caught her breath. 'Why don't you come with me, Dad?'

'I swore I'd never set foot in the place while Hamish lived,' he replied harshly. 'And I wouldn't want to see it while he's there. But what happens when he's gone will be a different matter. Don't worry about it, Jill! Take it as it comes. Just do the right thing now and you'll never regret it.

'Your mother didn't live long enough

to have any lasting joy, and missed the experience of seeing you grow up into the beautiful girl you are. I only hope you will have more than enough happiness in your life to compensate for what she missed.'

Jill nodded slowly, determined to face the challenge Fate was thrusting her way, and despite her reservations about the future, she was excited by the uncertainties of the situation . . .

* * *

The next three weeks passed quickly and the end of May brought Jill's holiday into reality. During the final week-end before she was due to go to Scotland, her mind became filled with doubt.

The trouble was that she had no idea what to expect. She knew nothing at all about her grandfather beyond the fact that he was an unforgiving man who had turned his back on his daughter, not even relenting when she died! And until now he had shown absolutely no interest in his only grandchild! Jill considered that fact and could not help wondering what kind of a reception she would receive at Crag House . . .

On Monday morning, she set out for the airport accompanied by her father, and became nervous as they awaited the time of departure. She felt strangely emotional, and kissed her father soundly when her flight was called.

'Phone me as soon as you get there.' He spoke hoarsely. 'Have a nice time, and if your grandfather is still the man he was then stand up to him! Don't let him bully you!

'Your mother never let him get the better of her and you're her daughter! You're like her in so many ways and I wouldn't be surprised that the sight of you will melt Hamish's heart, if he has one.'

Jill nodded.

'I'll phone you this evening. Take care!'

'I'll be all right.' He patted her shoulder.

She smiled and joined the other passengers on her flight to board the aircraft, then settled down for the comparatively short trip . . .

She had been given instructions for the journey in a second letter from her grandfather's solicitors and nothing had been left to chance. An itinerary had been laid out for her and she followed it closely.

The flight was soon over and leaving the airport, she took a train to the port where she would embark for the Isle of Inver. She looked around with interest when they reached the harbour. The weather was calm for early June and the sun was shining. Spring had been wet but was now just a fading memory, and excitement stirred in Jill as she looked to the future . . .

Boarding a small passenger boat, Jill hoped the sea was calm — she didn't consider herself a very good sailor. But the two-hour trip soon passed and the boat was eventually tied up at a stone quay where a number of small fishing boats were moored.

Her eyes glistened as she went ashore, looking around with great interest, aware that this scenery was just as her mother must have seen it. There were hills in the background, bleakly majestic, dominating the little harbour, and Jill, having lived most of her life in London, regarded them with awe.

But there was a touch of unreality in her mind, for none of this seemed to be real. After all the tales she had heard of Crag House, it was hard to believe that she was on her way to see her mother's birthplace!

She was excited now, and thoughts of her mother had strengthened in her mind. It was a sentimental attitude, but Jill relished it, and began to look forward to her first glimpse of the house that had once been home to her mother . . .

A black car was waiting on the quay, and the driver, a tall, long-faced man of middle-age, got out and approached her, touching his cap.

'Good afternoon. Miss Jill Telford?' he greeted.

'That's right,' Jill replied.

'I'm James Buchan, miss. If you'd get into the car I'll put your cases in the boot.' He had a very strong, Scottish accent. 'I hope you will enjoy your stay at Crag House.'

'Thank you.' Jill nodded determinedly. 'I'm sure I shall.'

He touched his cap and, moving away, Jill got into the car. Her luggage was put into the boot and then the man slid behind the wheel and put the car into gear.

The big vehicle moved smoothly forward, and Jill looked around as they drove through the town, sensing an atmosphere which struck her forcibly, for she knew that her mother must have come here often in the old days and had seen these very sights.

They left the town and drove along a country road.

Small cottages were nestling in the fine landscape, and the bare hills in the distance seemed to frown upon Jill as she studied them. At last she had come back to her grass roots, but now she had to face her grandfather with hardly an idea of to expect from this formidable old man or what attitude she should face him with . . .

2

Jill watched the scenery with interest on the drive across the island, until finally the car turned in between black wrought-iron gates and followed a winding track between tall trees that blotted out the sunshine.

She looked out of the car, saw a deep ravine only feet from the wheels, and caught the angry mutter of a rushing torrent that was cascading over dark rocks far below. She held her breath as the car lurched over what seemed a rather flimsy wooden bridge which swayed under the weight of the vehicle.

Minutes later they emerged from under the trees, and before her was the stark outline of a large house perched high on a lonely crag, starkly forbidding in the bright daylight. They approached quickly, bumping over the unfinished road until the car finally reached a paved courtyard.

Jill peered from the window of the car, eager for a first glimpse of Crag House. Thick ivy was clinging tenaciously to grey stone walls and there was a large bell hanging in a tower at the far end of the courtyard. She sighed, keenly aware of the silence that seemed to close in around her as she looked at the many tall windows. It was then she experienced an uncanny feeling that someone, somewhere was watching her.

The slam of the driver's door startled her and she alighted, looking around with interest, aware of emotion in the back of her mind as she gazed at her ancestral home.

This rugged pile of stonework had been a haven for the clan that lived on this island for centuries, and it was likely that much Campbell blood had been shed through the years in defending it. Doubtless the spirits of those ancestors lingered yet in the dusty corners and grey stones.

She approached the big, arched doorway, hardly able to contain her emotion, seeing at close hand the smooth walls and the worn steps leading up to the door, and she paused on the top step to reach out and touch the green moss that clung tenaciously to the crumbling mortar between the stones.

The atmosphere was brooding, as if the building knew it would survive any mortal who had the temerity to approach, and Jill drew a deep breath before reaching out to pull an iron ring set in the stone wall and start a quivering peal of harsh sound ringing through the still air.

She looked up at the arch overhead and saw, at the very top, a small, weather-worn gargoyle grinning stonily at her. It had the body of an animal, with blackened stone wings protruding from it, and the eroded face of an old man. Then the sound of a bolt being withdrawn attracted her attention and she turned back to the door as it was opened.

A thick-set face peered at her and there was enquiry in its expression. Then the door was opened wider and a man confronted Jill. His hair was thin and grey, his eyes narrowed, dark with suspicion. He was old, his tall frame stopped at the shoulders. In his prime she suspected he would have been quite powerful.

'Good afternoon. I'm Jill Telford. My grandfather is expecting me.' Jill's voice echoed slightly, and at her back she could hear James Buchan ascending the steps with her luggage, his breathing loud and whistling.

The door opened wider as a smile touched the man's lean, weather-darkened features. Then he made a little bowing motion.

'Welcome to Crag House, Miss Telford.' He spoke in a surprisingly soft voice. 'We've waited a long time to meet you! I'm Alec Seward, the butler. I hope you will enjoy your stay here.'

'Thank you!' Jill was pleasantly surprised by the warmth of his tone.

'Please, won't you come in?' He glanced past her at the approaching driver and added sharply, 'Leave the luggage here in the hall, Buchan.'

Jill crossed the threshold into a high, wide hall, and was immediately impressed by the oak-panelled walls and the massive, curving staircase. There were ancient weapons on display on the walls, and two suits of armour stood like sentinels on either side of the bottom step of the staircase. An unmistakable smell of age clung to the daunting atmosphere.

A woman emerged from a ground floor room. Tall and thin, she, too, was quite old, but her pale blue eyes were gleaming as she held out a hand in greeting while her face proclaimed genuine pleasure.

'This is my wife, Amena, who is the housekeeper here,' Seward told Jill. 'I don't have to introduce Miss Telford to you, Amena, do I?'

'Certainly not!' Amena Seward grasped Jill's hands and squeezed them. 'You're the image of your mother, my dear! It's uncanny how you resemble her, but that was to be expected. I wish you a happy stay here.'

'Thank you.' Jill smiled. 'I'm very excited.'

'I'll show you around when you've rested.' Amena was Scottish, her soft voice carrying the gentle richness of a Highland brogue. 'I'll show you to your room and you can refresh yourself. Alec will bring your luggage along.'

'How is my grandfather?' Jill enquired. 'I understand he doesn't keep very well these days.'

'He's not so bad!' Alec Seward picked up Jill's cases. 'The doctor saw him yesterday, and the only thing Hamish suffers from is age. But he's eager to meet you. I'll put your cases in your room before I report to him.'

He set off up the staircase with Jill and the housekeeper following.

'You've been given the room which was your mother's,' Amena informed her.

'My father said you knew my mother!'

'Indeed I did! It is such a long time ago now, but I remember her well. She was very beautiful, and so much in love with your father.'

'And, of course, you would have known my father, too!'

'I carried messages between him and your mother, although it might be better if your grandfather did not learn of that, even after all these years.' Amena paused on the stairs and looked into Jill's intent face. 'Your father has become very successful, and it is a tragedy that your mother did not live to see it. She did everything she could to help him.'

'She even gave up her family for him.' Jill's tone was serious.

'It may be difficult for you to understand why your grandfather was so strict.' Amena shook her head. 'But he was always a hard man! However, age has mellowed him and he is eager to see you.' She paused before adding in a slightly hushed tone, 'There will be two other guests while you are here. Owen and George Craig have been invited to meet you. They were your Aunt Fiona's stepsons. Fiona died about six years ago.'

'And Aunt Fiona married a Scot?' Jill queried.

'Yes. Donald Craig was a true Highlander.'

Jill shook her head as they continued, and when they reached the top of the stairs she paused with a gasp, for there was a portrait of a young woman on the wall where the light from a large window fell directly upon it.

'That must be my mother!' she exclaimed. 'I hadn't realised the resemblance between us was so apparent.'

'Yes!' Amena's voice was sad. 'I well remember when that portrait was painted. Your mother was a dear, dear lassie!'

'The photographs my father had of my mother are old and worn now — I never realised just how beautiful she was.' She gazed at the proud face in the picture, seeing herself in every line of countenance.

There were the same brown eyes, in which the artist had captured a hint of defiance that depicted such spirit and determination that made Jill, recognising it, catch her breath.

'Your grandfather has talked of nothing but your visit since you agreed to come. He's a very sorry man now, believe me. But he cannot turn back the clock and has to live with his conscience.'

'I suppose it seems much worse to him because Mother died when I was born, but that cannot be blamed on Grandfather. It might have happened had she stayed here.'

'I'm glad you have that attitude.' Amena nodded as they went on. 'It will help. But no-one would have blamed you had you decided to stay away.'

'I came because I think Mother would have wished it.'

Amena paused along the corridor

and fumbled with a bunch of keys before opening a door. Then she stepped aside to give Jill her first glimpse of the room that had been her mother's.

Jill paused in the doorway, her eyes misting over as she looked around, struck by the thought that her mother had been the last person to use this room.

'Nothing has been changed in here,' Amena said. 'We've kept it just the way your mother liked it. The colour scheme was her favourite, and the hair brushes on the dressing table are the ones she used.'

Jill's eyes blurred with emotion, and she fancied she could sense her mother's presence, certain that ghosts of the past haunted this room. Then she crossed to the tall window and looked out over smooth, green lawns and vivid flower beds, and it was as if her mother stood by her side, sharing the views she herself had known so many years before . . .

There was a single bed in the room, and antique furniture that gave atmosphere to the mustiness which Jill smelled. But it was her imagination that supplied the age, for the room was scrupulously clean, and Jill was entranced by it.

'Do you like it?' Amena enquired. 'I didn't want to put you in here but Hamish insisted. He thought you would want to use it.'

'And he's right.' Jill nodded. 'I'll be very happy in here.'

'I'll show you where the bathroom is. It doesn't adjoin your room, but it is only a little way along the corridor.'

Jill nodded and they went back into the corridor. The house had not been in any way modernised, that fact seeming to indicate much of her grandfather's old-fashioned character, Jill thought. But the building had obviously been well maintained.

'Do you employ many staff?' she asked.

'Buchan is the only one really — his

jobs are chauffeur and gardener!'
Amena shook her head. 'I can well
remember the days when there were a
dozen maids.'

'When shall I meet Grandfather?' Jill
wanted to get the ordeal over as soon as
she possibly could.

'Now, if you wish! But would you like
to have tea first?' Amena opened a door
to reveal a large bathroom. 'This is for
your own personal use. If you would
like to freshen yourself then I'll arrange
tea, and afterwards you can see your
grandfather.'

'Thank you. I'd like to change. Is
Grandfather confined to his bed? I
rather thought he would have met me at
the front door.'

Amena smiled.

'We had difficulty keeping him in bed
today. But the doctor says he must rest
because he was over-excited by the
thought of your arrival. However, I
don't think we'll be able to keep him
lying down when he learns you are here
at last. But try not to over-excite him. It

would be bad for him.'

'Meeting me could upset him?' Jill observed worriedly.

'Not in that way.' Amena smiled. 'Your visit will be a treat for him.'

Jill considered the situation as she went back to her room to change, and was able to feel an atmosphere closing in around her. She imagined there were many uneasy ghosts in this large house, and could only hope that her arrival would bring peace to some of them . . .

It was early evening before she met Hamish Campbell. Amena led her to a ground floor room and tapped at the door. Jill felt her nervousness increase as the housekeeper peered into the room.

'Your granddaughter is here, Mr Campbell,' Amena announced.

'Bring her in,' a quavering voice replied.

Amena stepped aside, smiling encouragement at Jill, who drew a steadying breath and braced her shoulders as she entered the room. She heard the sound of the door closing behind her and glanced round to see that the housekeeper had remained outside. Then she tilted her chin and went forward, her mind sated with emotion.

There was a large bed in the room, but it was unoccupied, and as Jill looked towards the window, she saw a man was seated in a high-backed chair. What struck her was his long, thin face which was utterly haggard with age, and the deep pallor in his hollow cheeks. He was wearing a dressing-gown, but its voluminous folds could not conceal his thin body.

'Hello, Grandfather!' Jill crossed the room to confront him, aware that his dark eyes were regarding her intently, much as an eagle watched its prey.

'So you are Jenny's daughter — my granddaughter!' Hamish held out his gnarled right hand. Despite its appearance the fingers were long and the palm large giving the impression that in his younger days he would have been a force to be reckoned with. But now his hands and wrists were skeletal, the clawlike hand he extended trembling uncontrollably.

Jill grasped his hand and squeezed it gently, a little surprised by the strength her grandfather displayed.

'Welcome to Crag House!' Hamish paused, then laughed. 'That sounds quite ridiculous after all these years, doesn't it? Especially after I banished your mother before you were even thought of.' He shook his head. 'I should have sent for you long ago. My stupid pride has been the immovable obstacle.' He shook his head, his dark eyes glinting with emotion.

'I'm happy to be here now.' Jill felt a lump in her throat. 'This was my mother's home and I'm glad of the opportunity to see it.'

'Your mother!' A sigh escaped him. 'Yes, we shall talk about her later! Did you have a good trip from London?'

'It was pleasant. I came most of the way by air, which didn't take long! And now that I'm here I am happy to be using my mother's room.'

'She was the last person to use it, which was so long ago, and yet I can recall the happy days when she was here.' His dark eyes seemed to burn with an inner fire as he regarded her. 'You're very much like your mother!'

'I hope the resemblance won't bring you too many unhappy memories.'

'I've been unhappy since the day she left! Now my regret is that I did not send for you before this. Please sit down. I want to know all about you. I have followed your father's career closely, and I am glad he found success. But I suspect he wouldn't forgive an old man for the past.'

'He is a forgiving man,' Jill defended stoutly.

'And you? How do you feel about me?'

'I have no bitterness! Although you sent Mother away it was not that which killed her. I feel sorry for you, Grandfather. I'm sure you would have relented, given time, but Mother died before your pride subsided.'

He nodded slowly.

'And that is all it was. Pride! How I've suffered for it! I cannot ease my conscience!'

'Please, try not to think about it,' Jill chided him gently. 'It's all in the past, and recalling it can only give you pain.'

'Unfortunately the past cannot be altered.' He shook his head. 'No-one knows better than I that what is done is done! But the past has become very important to me. I cannot get about much now, being confined either to my bed or a chair, and that is when my thoughts take over.

'It frustrates me that I have left it almost too late to make amends, which is why I have sent for you. But please do not think I am trying to salve my conscience! I am merely trying to rectify matters. You are my sole blood relation, and have certain rights which I've denied you until now.' His voice trailed off and he shook his head.

Jill saw suffering in his face and could

imagine what his life had become. He was torturing himself, and when the end came it might be a relief.

'I want to learn all about you over the next three weeks.' His voice cut into her thoughts. 'I shall be most interested in everything you have to say.'

'And will you tell me about my mother? I would dearly love to know about her childhood. There have been so many questions in my mind since I was old enough to think about her, and my father couldn't tell me much.'

'I'll welcome any question you care to ask. And I hope you will not be lonely here. I have invited your two cousins to provide company but they have not yet arrived. Owen and George Craig. They are not blood relations. Your Aunt Fiona married their father when they were children. They are nice young men, and were brought up here.'

'You're expecting them quite soon?'

'This evening!' He paused. 'How very much like your mother you are! She would have been very proud of you.'

'I wish we could have known each other!' Jill's blue eyes were bright, and she was finding it difficult to believe that this frail, old man could have acted so badly in the past.

But it was not for her to judge him, and if she could bring him some measure of peace during her stay then she would be happy. She felt she owed it to her mother's memory to do what she could.

'Perhaps we should now touch on business!' Hamish said.

'I'd rather not this evening,' she replied quickly. 'It's too soon.'

'Of course. We'll take our time.' He nodded. 'What do you think of Crag House?'

'It's beautiful. I was overwhelmed by the sight of it.'

'And how are the staff treating you?'

'Very well! Mrs Seward is very nice. She told me she knew my mother.'

'Indeed! And disloyally carried messages between your mother and father!' He shook his head, his gaze sliding past

Jill to study the scene outside the window, his eyes unblinking. 'She doesn't know I knew about that.'

Jill was relieved that his attitude had mellowed. She looked at him, saw his pleasure, and could not deny him the comfort of seeing her or blame him for the way he had acted.

The past was gone and so was her mother, and she could only try to ease the hurt he was still feeling over those unpleasant incidents of long ago. She clasped his hand tightly and he smiled.

'Thank you for coming,' he said. 'I am so very pleased to see you. But the excitement of awaiting your arrival has drained me of what little strength I possess.

'I must rest now, so perhaps you would leave me. And if Owen and George arrive this evening please welcome them. I'll see them in the morning.'

'Very well, Grandfather!' Jill turned away and walked to the door, where she paused, to look back at the thin, lonely figure by the big window.

He was sitting stiff and straight in his chair, gazing out of the window as if looking into his past, and pity stirred through her as she departed.

Amena appeared, and Jill guessed she had been waiting for her to finish.

'I'd like to telephone my father now,' she said.

Amena nodded.

'There's a telephone in the library. I'll show you where it is if you'd like to come with me.'

Jill followed the housekeeper and, when they entered the library, she paused to look around the massive room.

The walls were lined with books from floor to ceiling and there was a leather-covered writing desk placed to catch the light from the tall window. A chandelier was suspended from the ceiling, and the heavy atmosphere pervading the room made Jill shiver.

'The telephone is by the window,' Amena said. 'If there is anything you require, please ring.' She indicated a bell rope by the great fireplace.

'Thank you.' Jill went to the table and picked up the telephone as she sat in a large chair, half turning to look from the tall window that gave a view of the courtyard.

Amena departed and Jill dialled her London number. But there was no reply, and, as she hung up, she heard the sound of a vehicle arriving.

Glancing from the window she saw a black car stopping in front of the main entrance. She craned forward as two men alighted from the car, and saw the front door open as they ascended the steps.

Alec Seward appeared in the door-way, and Jill saw his lips moving as he greeted the newcomers, although she could not hear what was being said. But she saw the expressions of the two men change simultaneously, and could guess that the butler was passing on the news of her arrival.

The taller of the two scowled, his

brows drawing together, his whole manner exuding ill humour, and Jill was shocked as she realised that her arrival might not be welcomed.

The men entered the house, and when the door had closed, Jill caught her breath and turned away from the window, her mind stuck with the scowl she had witnessed.

These men were not related to her, and the thought arose that, possibly in ignorance of her existence, they had considered Crag House and all it contained as being theirs when Hamish died.

She suppressed a pang of intuition and steeled herself as a knock sounded at the library door, and she was aware of stark reality confronting her. Owen and George Craig were wasting no time in meeting her.

3

Seward opened the library door and peered in at Jill, who had moved to stand with her back to the fireplace.

'Miss Telford, your cousins have arrived. Would you like to see them now?'

'Yes, thank you.' Jill drew a deep breath. Her hands were trembling, and she clasped them together as the newcomers entered the room and advanced upon her with Seward in close attendance.

'This is Owen Craig.' Seward introduced the foremost of the two men.

Jill found herself facing a burly man who was hardly taller than herself. He was probably thirty years old, and his dark eyes gazed intently at her as he offered a hand. His grip seemed overstrong, as if he were subconsciously conveying his power. He was well dressed in a dark grey suit cut from excellent cloth.

'How do you do?' His voice was deep, and his slightly round face creased into a smile. But Jill noted that his eyes remained expressionless, alert, taking in her every detail.

'How do you do?' she responded, sensing an innate hostility in him, at the same time being aware that intuition was sounding an alarm in her mind as he backed away to permit his brother to be introduced.

'This is Owen's brother, George,' Seward continued.

Jill suffered a crushed hand from George Craig when they shook hands, and unobtrusively massaged her fingers while Seward departed and the Craigs seated themselves opposite her. Tension had filtered into her mind, as if unpleasant impressions were forming.

'It was something of a shock when we found out about you,' Owen said in a penetrating voice. The backs of his large hands and powerful fingers were almost covered in black hair, Jill noticed, and his brows were thick and shapeless, beetling over narrowed, brown eyes. He was a good-looking man in an over-large way, and oozed arrogance with every word and gesture.

Jill was filled with disquiet as first impressions consolidated in her mind. These men were not related to her, and she found herself wishing that they had not been invited to witness her first visit to the family home.

'We did not know you even existed until after you had been contacted,' volunteered George. His tone was gentler than his brother's but he was a replica of Owen, although slightly taller, and his features were more regular. Jill regarded him as passably good-looking.

'We had no idea that we had a half-cousin,' Owen remarked.

'But here you are.' George's tone hardened imperceptibly.

It was obvious to Jill that they both resented her turning up out of the blue.

'Where have you come from?' George continued.

'London.' Jill spoke firmly. 'I've always lived there.'

'And never came to see Grandfather!' Reproof sounded in Owen's tone.

'How could I, not knowing he existed until I heard from his solicitor just weeks ago!' Jill shrugged. 'My branch of the family was disowned.'

'I heard Aunt Jennifer was cut off for marrying your father.' George nodded. 'We are not blood relations you realise. Aunt Fiona was not our natural mother.'

'I had heard.' Jill nodded. 'And neither of you lives here now!'

Owen scowled.

'We live in Glasgow and cannot visit often. How long are you staying? Is this some kind of holiday?'

'I plan to spend three weeks here. Grandfather wanted to meet me.'

'After all this time.' George buttoned and unbuttoned his jacket. 'That sounds significant.'

'I'm afraid I don't understand,' Jill responded.

'Have you any idea why Grandfather wants us here during your visit?' Owen interrupted. 'Has he said anything to you?'

Jill shook her head.

'I've seen him only briefly. He was worn out with the excitement of my arrival.'

The two men exchanged glances, and Owen nodded as if her words confirmed some suspicion he had evolved. His dark eyes were inscrutable.

'Well,' he observed, 'I suppose all will become clear in good time! It's a pleasure to meet you, Jill.' He arose, motioning to George to do likewise. 'We shall return shortly. I would like to continue our conversation.'

George began to speak but Owen manoeuvred him to the door. Jill watched in silence as they departed, wondering what was in their minds.

They were rather intense, and she had the horrible feeling that they felt uncomfortable with her sudden appearance, realising that but for her they might have inherited the estate, and had probably expected to do so from the time they were old enough to consider such matters . . .

She went to a tall window to gaze out at the rugged moorland stretching away to the horizon, where it was purpled by the distance, a growing uneasiness slowly evolving in her mind, and she failed when she tried to shrug it off. Pacing the room, she considered the impressions they had made on her.

The brothers had welcomed her, albeit grudgingly, but some underlying intuitive sense had sent a warning to the forefront of her mind and she found herself hoping that they were not going to stay for the next three weeks. She went to the telephone to call her father, and her spirits rose when he answered.

'Jill! I'm so glad to hear from you!' he said. 'I've been thinking about you all day. How was the trip?'

'Quite good. No problems. How did

your appointment go?'

'Fine. But I don't want to talk about that at the moment. How did you find your grandfather?'

'Lively enough, although he's not very well! I like him, Dad. He's obviously mellowed since your time.'

'I'm glad to hear it! He was a tyrant in the old days. I hope you'll get along well with him.'

'I'm sure I shall. But so much has happened today!'

'Is anything wrong?' His tone was sharp.

'No! I'm just tired, I expect. It's been a long and very exciting day.'

'Has anything been said about you staying there permanently?'

'No! And I wouldn't agree to that if I were asked!'

'Well, don't worry about it.' He chuckled. 'Don't cross your bridges until you come to them, Jill. I'm sure you'll be able to face any problems that may come up, and we should be able to arrange the future to suit us both. If I'm able to get away at the week-end would you like me to come and see you? Do you need me to be there for you?'

'I'd love it!' Jill spoke eagerly, and, thinking of Owen and George Craig, she added, 'I might need someone on my side.'

'What does that mean?' His voice sharpened with suspicion. 'Are you all right, Jill?'

'Yes, of course!' She moistened her lips in an attempt to regain her composure. 'If you came, I'm sure you would get a warm welcome from Grandfather. He asked if I thought you would be able to come to terms with the past. How would you feel about meeting him after all these years?'

'As long as it made you happy! But I can't make any firm plans at the moment so call me later in the week, after you've settled in, and we'll discuss the situation then. I'm sure you want to get yourself sorted out first.'

'All right. I'll ring again in a few days. But do try to come up this week-end,

Dad! Goodbye!' Jill suppressed a sigh as she hung up, but felt better for having spoken to her father.

Looking around, she became aware that she was oppressed by the heavy atmosphere of the house and went to her room to fetch a coat with the intention of going out for a walk.

She moved quietly, not knowing exactly where Owen and George were and having no wish to alert them.

They would have rooms on this floor, she guessed, fetching a coat and putting on walking shoes. But when she peeped out into the corridor she had to duck back, for Owen was in the act of tapping on a bedroom door nearby.

Waiting with bated breath, she heard the door opening, and then Owen's penetrating voice sounded deeply along the dark passage.

'Why haven't you gone down to keep an eye on her?' he demanded. 'We have to stay close to her at all times. And you must be especially nice to her! Make an effort to get into her good books. Try to impress her!

'It looks like an uphill task, but remember what's at stake and that we have nothing to lose!'

'I keep telling you it will be a waste of time and effort,' George replied. 'She's young and attractive, and probably has a boyfriend somewhere.'

'So can you think of a better plan than mine?' Owen's voice took on an edge. 'Or are you prepared to let all this slip through our fingers?'

'I think we're too late!' Resignation sounded in George's tone. 'She's family to the old man and will inherit everything. You know what the Campbells are like! Her mother was disinherited because she married an Englishman! So you've got some rethinking to do, Owen. The only way we'll get anything now is if something untoward happens to her.'

'Well, we can hope, can't we?' Owen chuckled, and the sound sent an icy pang of fear down Jill's back.

'Come on, we made plans before we

arrived and we've got to stick to them. Go down and see what she's doing. One of us has to be in her company whenever she's out of her room.'

Jill closed the door quietly as footsteps sounded in the corridor. Pressing against the door, she considered what she had overheard, and felt frightened. Her impressions had been correct!

The Craigs had expected to inherit Crag House on the death of her grandfather but her arrival had ruined all their plans.

But why would they want to watch her closely? And what plans had they laid before arriving? She suppressed a shiver as she feared that she might not like the answers to those illuminating questions . . .

What was she to do now? She could not remain shut in her room while they were here. She would have to communicate with them, if only to discover their intentions.

She crossed to the french window

and looked out upon a narrow veranda that ran the length of the house, and a sigh of relief escaped her. Here was a way out which would conceal her from the eyes of her so-called cousins!

Leaving the room, she walked quietly along the veranda and descended the steps at the far end, which took her towards the rear of the house.

Afraid of being spotted from the big, front windows, she followed a narrow, gravelled path to the rear and came upon the large, kitchen gardens. A high wooden gate was set in a massive brick wall and, passing through the gateway, she found herself at the start of a path that led away from the house to lose itself in the emptiness of the moor.

She followed it for about a mile, then reached a clump of firs, where she paused in their shadows to enjoy the views of the rugged countryside while remaining out of sight of anyone who might look in her direction from Crag House.

The evening was fine, the blue sky

dotted with fleece-like clouds that drifted on a faint breeze.

Jill sighed with pleasure, but her thoughts were far from pleasant as she thought about what she had overheard at the house. Her expression became troubled and her forehead wrinkled as she frowned.

So Owen and George Craig considered her an enemy! She had dashed their hopes of inheriting Crag House! But what could they do about her? She tried not to think too much about that.

It was a development she could have done without, she realised, and a restlessness seized her. Moving out along the path, she followed it into the moor, enjoying the solitude and peacefulness surrounding her.

Lost in thought, Jill did not realise how far she walked, and the path seemed to go on for ever.

When she finally reached a small copse of tall trees she decided to turn and retrace her steps, but was startled when a large, black dog sprang out from the undergrowth, barking excitedly.

She instinctively recoiled. Her foot twisted on a tuft of grass which sent her sprawling headlong, and she fell heavily. Bemused by the shock of the incident, by the time she regained her presence of mind the dog was standing over her, wagging its tail and licking her face.

Jill laughed as she patted the dog's head.

'Hello. Where did you come from?'

The animal licked at her even more furiously, and Jill grasped its collar and tried to hold it off.

'At least you're friendly!' she observed. 'But you must let me get up.'

She tried to get up, but when she put weight on her left ankle a stab of pain shot through it and she fell back, grasping the offending limb until the pain subsided.

She knew the dog was watching her, its head to one side, perhaps wondering what kind of game she was playing.

Examining her ankle, Jill groaned

when she saw how it had swollen, and for a few moments she wondered if it were broken. But she could move the joint and decided it was only sprained.

Trying to get up once more she realised that she could not put weight on the ankle.

'I think I have a problem!' she said to the dog. 'It wouldn't matter so much if I had four legs like you, but I'm a long way from home and can't walk. Do you have any ideas? Is your owner nearby?'

The dog cocked its head and wagged its tail, brown eyes gleaming. Then a distant whistle sounded and the animal whirled, moving like a black streak in the direction of the whistle.

Jill pushed herself up, balancing with her left foot off the ground, and hopped to the edge of the copse in the direction the dog had taken. She leaned thankfully against a tree.

The dog was in the distance, about two hundred yards away, darting around a tall figure coming along the path. A sigh of relief escaped Jill for she had begun to have visions of being stranded on the moor long after dark.

But then the man turned and began to retrace his steps, and she caught her breath.

She called loudly in the hope of attracting the man's attention, but his back remained resolutely turned towards her and she closed her mouth again, for even the dog failed to hear her voice.

She wondered why the animal had been so far ahead of its master, and why the man had not kept better control of it.

She decided to call again, but realised her voice could not carry that distance, and concern began to creep over her, knowing she was at least two miles from Crag House and unable to put one foot in front of the other. She glanced up at the sky and was perturbed to see signs of the approaching night showing in the east.

Looking around carefully, she realised that the stranger and the dog were apparently the only other living creatures able to help her.

Then she heard a series of shrill whistles and, returning her attention to the man and dog, her heart skipped a beat when she saw the dog now running towards her, patently ignoring the calls of its master, who was again facing Jill's direction.

The dog ran on determinedly, and Jill guessed it was returning for her, as if it had suddenly remembered their encounter and realised she had been hurt because of it.

She hobbled forward some yards to get clear of the trees and began to wave madly. The dog was still running towards her, and now, she saw with relief, the man was following swiftly.

Moments later the dog arrived. Jill sank to the ground, the animal's greeting being so exuberant she was almost knocked off balance. She patted the animal, having difficulty preventing herself being licked all over again.

'So you suddenly remembered me,

did you?' she demanded. 'You shouldn't have gone off like that, leaving a damsel in distress!' She narrowed her eyes, looking for the man, and moments later he arrived, his rugged face set in a frown.

He was tall and big-boned, in his middle twenties, his powerful figure dressed in expensive-looking tweeds. His face was somewhat shaded by the peak of a flat cap.

'I don't believe this!' he greeted while still some distance away. 'Dirk never disobeys me, and when he refused to heed my whistle I guessed something was wrong.'

'And you're right,' Jill agreed. 'I'm in a bit of bother, I'm afraid! I called when I saw you, but you were too far away to hear.'

'What's wrong? Have you hurt yourself?' He had very attractive features, Jill could not help noticing. His dark hair was mid length, and quite curly in an unruly way around his ears.

His jacket was undone, his white

shirt open at the neck, and his face and hands were deeply tanned. But it was his clear, brown eyes which held Jill's attention. They were bright and alive, filled with appreciation and boldness as he gazed at her.

Jill explained what had happened, and he shook his head and sighed before calling a sharp command to the dog, who instantly sank to the ground and lay motionless, its chin upon its paws and dark eyes fixed on Jill.

'Dirk can be a bit dramatic,' he commented, dropping to his knees beside Jill and taking her left foot in his capable hands. He examined her ankle, and he pressed his lips together when he saw the swelling that had arisen.

'Have you tried to stand on this?' His dark eyes were glistening when he looked up, and Jill caught her breath, for his friendliness was a welcome change after her meeting with Owen and George Craig.

'I can't put it on the ground,' she replied. 'I hopped clear of the trees in an attempt to attract your attention, but that is as far as I can go.'

'Where do you live? You're certainly not local anyway.'

'I'm staying at Crag House.'

'Crag House!' His voice sharpened imperceptibly, and Jill frowned as she detected an undercurrent in his tone.

'What's wrong with Crag House?' she countered.

'I'm very sorry. I shouldn't have used that tone. I was surprised by your answer, that's all. Are they taking guests at Crag House now?'

'I am a guest there, but not one of the paying kind. I'm Jill Telford. Hamish Campbell is my maternal grandfather!'

His rugged face showed surprise.

'Well,' he observed. 'It just goes to show! I always thought Hamish was the last of his line!' He produced a pen, then searched in his pockets for something on which to write.

Jill watched in surprise. His face was intent, and as he finished writing he looked up at her, taking her by surprise, meeting her gaze squarely with his keen brown eyes. She felt a stab of emotion at the impact of his gaze, and, for a moment, was unable to look away from him. But he turned his attention to the dog.

'Here, Dirk!' he commanded, and the dog leaped to his side, tail wagging. He folded the slip of paper and fastened it in the dog's collar, then patted the animal's head. 'Find Sarah!' he ordered briskly. 'Go home, Dirk!'

The dog turned instantly and set off to run in the direction Jill had seen master and dog walking. She watched it for some moments, then looked at the man, who was watching the dog intently.

'I've written a note to my sister, asking her to bring the Land-Rover here,' he explained. 'We shall have to wait about fifteen minutes.'

'Will Dirk go straight home?'

'Oh, yes. It's not the first time he's carried a message in his collar. In fact, he's almost as fast as pigeon post! I'm Robert Cameron, by the way. I farm around here, and the family home is just beyond the ridge over there.

'It was fortunate I was walking in this area or you could have been stranded here until they missed you at Crag House.'

'If you hadn't come in this direction Dirk wouldn't have knocked me off my feet,' she observed, 'and I wouldn't have injured my ankle.'

'That's true!' He nodded and sat down on the ground beside her, his nearness setting off a spark of indefinable emotion in Jill. 'I'm sorry we have caused you all this trouble.'

'It was my fault as much as Dirk's,' she said magnanimously. 'He didn't do it deliberately. I was surprised by his appearance, and fell before realising what was happening.'

'I don't understand. Dirk is a one-man dog and doesn't usually make a fuss of people, especially strangers. Even Sarah can't get close to him at times, and she always sees to him at mealtimes.'

'Maybe he thought I had something to eat.' Jill laughed.

He smiled, but quickly sobered.

'Weren't you warned it's dangerous on the moor unless you're accustomed to it?

'You should have been accompanied. If Dirk hadn't suddenly remembered you it's likely you would have been out here until a search was organised, which would probably have been in the morning. Did you tell anyone at Crag House that you intended walking out here?'

'No!' Jill thought of the way she had sneaked out, and shook her head.

His face was grave.

'You can't take liberties with the moor for it has a nasty way of getting back at you when you least expect it.' He smiled then and changed the subject. 'Is this your first time at Crag House? I haven't seen you around before.'

Jill explained something of the situation, and he listened in silence until she ended.

'Of course, the story of your mother and father is well known!' he observed. 'It's a pity some Highland families are so rigid in their attitudes.' He paused. 'Have you met Owen and George Craig yet?'

'Yes.' Jill kept her tone steady. 'They arrived this afternoon. I think the news of my existence was a shock to them.'

He frowned, lifting his gaze to the distance while Jill took the opportunity to study his profile. He was incredibly handsome! She liked his ruggedness, and could not help comparing him with the hostile Owen and George. A shiver touched her as she thought about them.

Before the arrival of the brothers she had been excited by the prospect of staying in the house where her mother was born, but now the whole concept seemed tainted somehow, and she realised that she was reluctant to return to Crag House.

'Ah! Here comes the Land-Rover!' he exclaimed suddenly, interrupting her thoughts. 'We'll soon have you back at Crag House!'

'Thank you! I'm sorry to be the cause of so much trouble!' Jill watched the approaching Land-Rover.

Robert Cameron got to his feet and waved to attract the driver, and soon the vehicle drew up nearby and a vivacious brunette leaped out, her beautiful face illuminated by curiosity. Seeing Jill, she paused to survey the scene.

'What's happened?' she demanded. 'When Dirk arrived with the note I began to imagine all kinds of things.'

'It's not serious, Sarah.' Robert explained the situation. 'Mind you, it could have become serious if Dirk hadn't remembered about Jill.' He smiled at Jill, and she felt a warmth spread through her at his use of her name. 'This is my sister, Sarah,' he continued. 'Sarah, this will surprise you. This is Jill Telford, Hamish

Campbell's granddaughter!'

Jill saw the girl's surprise, but Sarah smiled and came to shake hands, then squatted beside Jill to examine the ankle while her brother explained the circumstances of the accident.

'You're lucky, Jill,' he said, watching his sister. 'Sarah is a trained nurse. She'll run the rule over you before we take you home.'

'The ankle is badly sprained.' Sarah looked into Jill's eyes. 'You'll have to keep your weight off it for at least a week, which is not good news if you have just arrived with the intention of exploring the area.' She looked up at her brother.

'Get the first aid box out of the Land-Rover, Robert, and I'll bandage the ankle. I think you should see a doctor as soon as possible, Jill.

'And if you plan to stay for any length of time then I hope we'll see something of you. We don't get many new faces visiting us round here.'

'That's kind of you!' Jill warmed to

70

the girl immediately, whose friendly tone had already cemented her first impressions. 'It'd be nice to be able to make some friends.'

'Because you may end up living here?' Sarah demanded. 'You are Hamish Campbell's only blood relation, aren't you?'

'I don't suppose Jill has the remotest idea of what her future holds,' Robert interrupted. 'And it wouldn't do to speculate!

'But while she is here we must do what we can to welcome her into the community, sparse though it is.'

The sound of horse's hoofs suddenly became apparent and Jill turned her head to see a rider galloping towards them.

She recognised Owen Craig and her heart sank. Looking at Robert, she could see he was frowning as he watched the rider approach.

'What's going on here?' Owen demanded when he reined up beside the Land-Rover. 'Has there been an accident?'

'Nothing we can't handle,' Robert replied, and Jill was surprised by the hostility in his voice.

'I'm looking for a girl,' Owen continued, unaware of Jill sitting on the ground. 'Hamish Campbell's grand-daughter!'

'Miss Telford is here, and quite all right,' Sarah interrupted.

Owen frowned and, spotting Jill, sprang from the saddle and went over to where she was sitting on the grass.

'What happened?' he demanded. 'Are you all right, Jill? Why didn't you let us know you intended leaving the house?

'Surely you know that it's not safe to wander alone on the moor! You had only to mention you wanted to look around and I'd have been only too happy to escort you.'

'I wanted to be my myself!' Jill spoke distantly. 'You forget that I've never actually seen my mother's birth-place before.'

Owen's dark eyes narrowed as he nodded slowly.

'I'd better ride back to the house and let them know what's happened. They were ready to send out search parties when we noticed you'd gone.' He turned abruptly, went back to his horse and rode away.

Jill sighed and looked at her companions.

'Obviously I was soon missed,' she observed. 'But I needed to make a point. When I met Owen and George, I sensed they could take over my life with their attentiveness. That's why I came out alone. I have to start as I mean to go on.'

'And a good thing, too.' Sarah sniffed. 'Those two can be quite overpowering.' She bandaged Jill's ankle expertly and smiled as she got up. 'You will have to rest the ankle, but after a few days it should be as good as new.

'When you're able to get about again why don't you come over and see me? Having someone around should deter Owen and George.'

'Thank you!' Jill nodded. 'That

would be great. I'll take you up on it as soon as I'm feeling better.'

'And now we'd better get you home.' Robert's face was impassive as he picked up Jill as easily as if she were a child and carried her to the waiting vehicle. He settled her inside and sat with her, leaving Sarah to drive.

Jill leaned back and tried to relax, her mind vibrant with fleeting impressions. She was keenly aware of how close Robert was and it made her feel secure, especially when she thought about her cousins and what they were planning between them.

She had been so excited about visiting Crag House but now that visit had been overshadowed by a fear she couldn't quite place.

4

By the time Sarah's Land-Rover reached Crag House, a warm friendliness had grown between Jill and Sarah, while the close presence of Robert gave Jill a sense of comfort which helped the way she was feeling about this trip.

But she dreaded seeing Owen and George again! She suppressed a sigh as Sarah stopped the vehicle in front of the main entrance and Robert sprang out. He turned to pick up Jill as she tried to get out herself.

'It's better that I carry you!' he said with a smile.

'I'm sorry to be such a nuisance,' Jill replied, enjoying the sensation of his strong arms around her.

'It could have been much worse,' Sarah said, ascending the steps ahead of them. She reached out to ring the doorbell but the door was already opening, and Jill saw Owen Craig in the doorway, with George standing nearby. Both men were frowning, and Jill experienced a tremor of intuition as she looked at them.

'I was just saying,' Sarah observed. 'Jill has a badly-sprained ankle, but it could so easily have been much worse.'

'I hope we can keep this from Hamish!' Owen snapped. 'We don't want anything upsetting him in his present state of health!'

Robert walked forward with Jill in his arms and her feet almost struck Owen in the chest since he made no attempt to move out of the doorway until the last possible moment.

Robert crossed the threshold, and Jill realised she was gripping him around the neck with all her strength. He glanced down at her, his face harsh, but he smiled when he met her gaze. His brown eyes seemed depthless, gleaming with a blend of several emotions.

'Where to?' he asked generally. 'It's

been a long time since I last set foot in Crag House!'

'The library, please!' Jill said. 'It's quite comfortable in there.'

Owen hurried ahead and opened the library door before stepping aside — Jill was puzzled by his willingness to help. Robert carried Jill into the library and set her down gently on a leather couch by the window.

He smiled as he straightened up, and Jill had to bite her lip in order to stay calm. She knew that very soon, Robert and Sarah would go, leaving her alone with Owen and Craig.

'Thank you,' she said. 'You've been really kind.'

Sarah came to Jill's side and examined her ankle again, touching it gently and shaking her head.

'It will be all right so long as you keep your weight off it for a few days,' she decided. 'Would you like me to come and look at it tomorrow?'

'Yes, please, if you're sure you don't mind.' Jill's eyes were pleading as she met Sarah's gaze, and the girl nodded.

'Not at all — it's probably best.'

'I shall have the doctor in to look at Jill's ankle so there will be no need for you to bother,' Owen said sharply.

'I don't need a doctor!' Jill retorted. 'It's only a sprain!'

★ ★ ★

Sarah and Robert left a few minutes later and Sarah waved from the doorway as Robert glanced back over his shoulder, smiling in a way that made Jill want to get up and run after him.

George saw them to the door, and Owen's rasping voice brought Jill back to earth with a crash.

'You should have had more consideration,' he said. 'Grandfather's not up to dealing with any incidents like this. It's not good enough, you know. He asked the two of us to come here so we could look out for you but at the first opportunity you get yourself into all kinds of trouble! Perhaps in future you'll think before you act!

'Quite apart from that, I know for a fact that Grandfather doesn't like the Camerons. If he knew Robert and Sarah Cameron had set foot in Crag House I hate to think what would have happened! There was a lot of bad blood between Grandfather and the Cameron family many years ago and they've never got over it.'

'I'm sorry if you think I've caused trouble,' Jill replied firmly. 'But although Grandfather brought you here with the best of intentions, I am on holiday and quite able to look after myself. I certainly don't need an escort! And I'd rather find my own way around, thank you!'

'Grandfather won't like it if you make friends with the Camerons!'

'I've already told him that whatever happened in this house before my arrival is none of my business, and that applies to the Camerons as well as my mother. I'm beginning as I mean to go on, Owen. I'm quite capable of picking my own friends and I won't put up with interference from anyone no matter what their opinions are.'

'Look, I don't want to fall out with you before we really get to know each other but don't you think it would be better not to upset Grandfather?'

'I don't think that would honestly happen! But there is only one way to find out!' Jill pushed herself up from the couch and hobbled towards the door.

'Where are you going?' Owen demanded in alarm.

'To see Grandfather and let him know what's going on! If he thinks I'm in the wrong then I'll discuss it with him!'

'Whatever you do, don't upset him!'

'He's tougher than you think, Owen, and would take a lot of upsetting,' Jill responded.

She hobbled out of the room with Owen following closely, and speaking severely all the way to the door of

Hamish's room. But the instant she tapped at the door he turned abruptly and departed. Jill gazed after him, feeling very uneasy.

Then she opened the door in response to Hamish's voice and found her grandfather propped in his chair by the window, gazing at the landscape outside.

'What's happened to your leg?' Hamish's thin voice crackled in the silence of the room.

'I had a small accident!' Jill gave an account of her outing on the moor. 'It's lucky that Robert Cameron was on hand to help me out.' She went on to explain how he had then sent for his sister. 'It turned out Sarah is a trained nurse, so I fell into the right hands.'

'Hm! I doubt if Cameron's hands are the right ones! But I suppose you weren't to know that I am not the best of friends with any member of the Cameron family. It's a story that goes back many years.'

'I can't understand it — I found

Sarah and Robert quite friendly! Did you have some kind of argument with them?'

'With their father! Many years ago he tried to steal a piece of land on our boundary, and never forgave me when I went to court and proved my title.'

'Many years ago?' Jill smiled. 'Before Robert and Sarah were born?'

'Yes. I suppose it was.' Hamish's tone softened imperceptibly.

'Then you don't actually have any argument with Robert and Sarah?'

'No!' He realised where the conversation was leading.

'So you won't actually mind if I decide to stay friends with them?'

Hamish shook his head slowly, his narrowed eyes upon Jill's intent face.

'That means you don't accept Owen and George in the rôle I hoped they would play?' he replied at length.

'I'm too independent,' she replied, 'and don't make friends quickly. I need to be on my own for a few days to give myself time to take in these new surroundings gently and get used to this situation. The thing is, I have a grandfather I never knew I had and also I'm in the place where my mother grew up — a mother I never knew either.

'I never knew her so I never grieved for her when I was old enough to understand that she had died at my birth, but I missed her badly over the years, and I need time in which to get used to all these new ideas.'

Hamish nodded.

'Forgive me for not realising the effect all this would have on you. If it would be better, I'll send Owen and George back to Glasgow to leave you in peace. But they were interested when I told them you were coming, and that's why I invited them.'

Jill shook her head.

'I wouldn't want to drive them away! I just want you to understand my feelings.'

'I do understand. I made a mistake, for which I apologise. I am very happy with the situation as it is, and will support you in everything you do. Don't give it a second thought.

'Go out and explore and enjoy yourself. Get used to the idea that this is your family home.

'My one regret is that I am too old now to come with you.' He lapsed into silence and averted his face from Jill to gaze from the window.

She went to his side and placed a hand on his shoulder.

'I'm so sorry, Grandfather,' she said softly. 'I know we can't change the past but maybe in the future we can avoid making the same mistakes.'

'Ay!' He reached across with a gnarled hand to grasp her hand and press it gently.

'I've learned that lesson well, but the understanding came much too late for some people!'

'I spoke to Father on the telephone!' Jill changed the subject abruptly. 'He may be able to come up from London at the week-end.'

'Come here?' Hamish sat upright.

'And is that what he wants?'

'Certainly, if you made him welcome!'

'Then let's not waste the opportunity!'

'Are you sure you don't mind me being here, Grandfather?' she asked anxiously. 'It must be a traumatic time for you, having me here as a constant reminder of the past.'

'Don't give it a second thought,' he replied. 'You're like a breath of fresh air, and my deepest regret is that I did not send for you years ago.'

Jill patted his shoulder and turned to leave the room, her thoughts over-burdened by her own emotional turmoil.

She went up to her room, filled with thoughts about the events of the day, her bad impressions of Owen and George made more bearable by the pleasure she had gained by meeting Robert and Sarah.

But her main reservations were about her grandfather. Hamish was undoubtedly suffering badly from a troubled conscience, and she wished she could find a way to alleviate his agony.

Her thoughts were interrupted by Owen appearing suddenly from his room as she passed by the half-open door.

It was obvious he had been waiting for her, and she looked into his set face and brooding eyes and experienced a spasm of alarm.

What she had overheard him saying to his brother lay heavily on her mind, and now she was getting some feedback from it. She had to prepare herself for trouble.

'How did you find Grandfather?' he demanded.

'Very well!' She smiled. 'He's quite happy that I intend making my own friends, and he's even pleased that my father is planning to visit here at the week-end.'

Owen frowned as he watched Jill intently.

'Grandfather has sworn that your father would never set foot in Crag

House again!' He pressed his lips together. 'He must be mellowing in his old age! But I'm happy for you! This must be quite a daunting situation for you to face on your own.'

'But all's well that ends well!' Jill turned abruptly and went to seek the sanctuary of her room . . .

5

Jill found it difficult to sleep that night. Her mind was overwhelmed by the events of the last day, and the atmosphere of the big, old house seemed suffocating with its memories sealed into the very fibre of the building.

She couldn't help think about her mother, and she wondered if she would ever be able to come to terms with what had occurred many years before under the dark roof of Crag House.

Eventually she did slip into an uneasy slumber, and only woke when an unnatural sound pierced her mind.

She sat up in the semi-darkness, looking around while trying to work out what had disturbed her.

Faint moonlight was shining in at the tall window, filling the room with silvery shadows. Then she heard scratching sounds, and her breath caught in her throat as fear enveloped her.

At first she thought it might have been a trapped rat, but the sound was moving slowly and seemed to be coming from the inner wall.

Sliding out of bed, she winced as her sprained ankle took her weight. She moved slowly towards the big fireplace, where, during the daylight hours, she had noticed a poker standing to one side.

Grasping the poker, she hobbled to the source of the noise and pressed her ear against the cold surface of the wall, immediately picking up tapping and slithering noises which sounded like nothing she'd ever heard before.

Jill steeled her faltering nerves and hurried to the door to lock it. She switched on the light and looked around the room. Now the noises were fainter but still audible, and she crossed to the bedside cabinet to check the time on her wrist watch. Four a.m.!

She stared at the wall, wondering

what was in the next room, which she had been told was unoccupied. But she didn't have the nerve to check it out. Not that she believed there was some kind of strange beast prowling around! But fear of the unknown gripped her and she got back into bed and sat huddled up, trying to come to terms with the disturbance and wondering at its source.

Gradually the noises faded away until it was silent again, and she slid down the bed and lay listening intently, her mind alert and every nerve in her body on edge.

But the silence continued while she remained in a state of frozen expectation, and when she glanced at her watch again the hands were pointing to five a.m.

She sighed and tried to relax, forcing her mind to accept the prospect of more sleep, but she dared not switch off the light and lay drowsing until the sun began to creep in through the window . . .

★ ★ ★

It was eight a.m. when she finally decided to go down to the dining-room for breakfast, but first she paused at the door of the room where the noises had sounded earlier.

Trying the door, she found it locked, and frowning, she descended the staircase and entered the dining-room, where Owen and George were already eating. Both men rose to greet her, and Jill took her place opposite them, shaking out the napkin that sat on her plate.

'Did you sleep well?' Owen enquired, his dark eyes expressionless as he regarded her.

'Yes, thanks,' she replied, having decided not to mention the disturbance.

'Did the atmosphere of the house bother you?' George did not look up, and seemed absorbed with buttering his toast.

'It always takes me a day or two to become accustomed to the atmosphere

here. It seems suffocating at times but I always seem to notice the little things that most people miss!'

'I like the atmosphere!' Jill countered. 'This is where my mother was born, remember! And it was her home for a long time! If there are any little things to be noticed, I'm sure I would notice them!'

'They do say the house is haunted.' Owen smiled. 'But so, apparently, are a lot of old houses, and I don't believe in ghosts!'

'Neither do I!' Jill smiled at Amena as the housekeeper appeared with her breakfast, and, while she ate, it crossed her mind that maybe Owen and George were trying to frighten her — as she was frightened last night. She shook her head slowly, surely not even they could stoop that low?

'How is your ankle this morning?' George asked solicitously.

'It's going to take a while to heal,' she replied.

'That's a pity.' George pushed his

plate to the side. 'I was hoping for the opportunity to show you around. But if you can't walk, I won't be able to give you a tour of the estate.' Despite his words he seemed relieved, and he glanced at Owen as he got up. 'So I think I'll just pop into town. There are some things I want to get.'

He left quickly, and Jill glanced at Owen's face, knowing that if they were planning something, Owen would be the one behind it.

'I suppose your friends will be coming round this morning,' Owen observed. 'You do realise that Grandfather won't be at all happy.'

'You mean Robert and Sarah! Yes. They'll be coming! They're very nice people. And Grandfather won't mind — I've already talked to him about that and everything is fine as far as he's concerned.'

'And he didn't tell you they couldn't come here?'

'Why should he? He doesn't have to see them!'

Owen got up, excusing himself, and Jill gazed after him as he left. Why did Grandfather have to invite them while she was there?

She could have done without all the aggravation. And what if one of them had been responsible for the noises that had disturbed her in the middle of the night?

Amena appeared and began clearing the table, her pale, blue eyes filled with an unfathomable expression as she looked at Jill.

'Did you sleep well last night?' she asked.

'Not really. I suppose I should tell you that the strangest thing happened . . . '

Jill described what had occurred and saw Amena's expression harden. The woman threw a quick glance at the door, as if she was afraid she might be overheard.

'That's very odd!' she agreed. 'The room next to yours is empty, and the empty rooms are kept locked. I'm the only one with keys!'

'I checked the door myself!' Jill tried to sound casual. 'But the sounds lasted for quite a while. Is the house haunted, Amena?'

'Don't go getting any silly ideas!' Amena met Jill's gaze. 'As for rats or mice!' She shook her head. 'The house is checked regularly, and we keep all the pests under control.' She paused before asking, 'You weren't frightened, were you? If you like, I'll sleep in that room next door to you for a few nights, just to set your mind at rest.'

'No. It's all right! I don't want to put you to any trouble.'

'I'll talk to Alec and see what he thinks!' Amena gathered up the crockery and put it on a tray. 'We'll see that you're not disturbed again.'

'I'm not worried about it, just a bit curious.' Jill got from the table to hobble to the door, and paused when Alec appeared. She sat down while Amena told her husband about the noises, all the time watching the butler's face. But Alec was giving nothing away, and shook his head.

'In an old house like this there are bound to be things that bump and creak,' he said, 'and when you've been here a few days you'll get used to it. You don't look like the kind of girl who's easily scared.'

'What does that mean?' Jill frowned. 'Do you think someone might be trying to scare me?'

'Not at all! It's just a figure of speech, miss. You do have a lot on your mind, and it'll take a while to get used to the old place.'

Jill smiled, knowing she would have to pay close attention to everything that went on in future.

'How is Grandfather this morning?'

'As well as yesterday,' Amena said, 'which is the best we can hope for.'

'I'm just going to the library,' Jill said and rose to her feet, 'and I'm expecting Sarah Cameron to call some time this morning.'

'I'll show her in when she arrives,'

Amena promised.

Jill began to read some of the books, glad that George had gone out and Owen was leaving her alone.

An hour later there was a knock at the door and Amena appeared, followed by Sarah Cameron.

'How's the ankle today?' Sarah asked. 'Shall I take a look at it?'

'It's still swollen!' Jill pulled off her slipper and Sarah sat down to examine it.

'It looks quite painful. It would be better if you let a doctor look at it, so I've already called the local surgery.

'We can drop in any time before noon and Dr Galloway will be there. I can drive you there if you like and then we could go on a sight-seeing tour. We can have lunch at the farm, and then decide what to do with the rest of the day. You're on holiday so you won't want to be stuck in here like an invalid.'

'Definitely not!' Jill agreed. 'It sounds like a great idea — I was just wondering what to do with myself.'

'That's settled then. Robert was asking for you and he said he'd try to pop in for lunch if he gets his work finished on time.'

'I'm not putting you to any trouble, am I?' Jill said worriedly.

'Not at all.' Sarah smiled. 'I'm just glad to see a new face around the place. How are you getting on with your cousins?'

'Not very well to be honest. Grandfather invited them to keep me company but they're taking it a bit too far.' Jill shook her head. 'I can't seem to turn round without bumping into them. But I had a word and hopefully now, they'll just leave me to it.'

'I know exactly what you mean.' Sarah nodded. 'Robert and I were brought here as company for Owen and George when they first arrived.

'I managed about three visits then cried off, but Robert stuck it out for quite a while, until Owen began to make his life a misery, and finally, there was a fight between them and Robert never came again.'

'I see!' Jill nodded. 'I could tell there was something between them when Owen rode up yesterday. And from what I've seen of Owen and George I'd say Owen was the ring leader in their little gang.'

'That's about right.' Sarah nodded. 'You mustn't let them get to you if you want to survive here!' She paused. 'Sorry, I didn't mean that literally.'

'I know what you mean!' Jill struggled to her feet. 'I'll get my shoes and bag, then I'm ready to leave. I'll just look in on Grandfather before I go, and let Amena know where I'm going to be today.'

'There's no rush,' Sarah replied with a smile. 'You are on holiday!'

'Yes — that's something I've almost forgotten,' Jill said with a frown.

6

Jill enjoyed her day more than she expected to. Sarah was great company, and after they visited the local surgery, where Jill found out that her ankle was no more than a bad sprain, Sarah whisked her off on a tour, showing her the well-known landmarks and giving her some history at the same time.

Jill forgot about the tensions at Crag House, and by the time Sarah drove to the farm where she and Robert lived, a close friendship seemed to be forging itself between them.

Jill was looking forward to seeing Robert again. She knew he'd made quite an impression on her.

Reaching the farm, a large, grey-stone building with many tall windows, Sarah parked in front of the entrance and helped Jill up to the house. Robert opened the door as they reached it, almost as if he had been awaiting their arrival, and his warm welcome filled Jill with pleasure.

'How are you feeling this morning?' he asked, offering her an arm, which Jill grasped firmly as she favoured her injured foot.

'We've seen Dr Galloway and he says it's no worse than a bad sprain,' Sarah said. 'Is lunch ready, Robert? I could eat a horse!'

'I'm afraid it's only a casserole,' Robert countered with a smile, and Jill laughed happily, enjoying the friendly atmosphere.

It wasn't something she'd experienced with Owen and George around. Robert was very helpful, prepared to fetch and carry for her, and when she protested that she had to do things for herself and not pretend she was an invalid, he remonstrated firmly, the ghost of a smile on his lips.

'But I feel responsible for your injury. My dog caused the accident, and the least I can do is give you a hand while you're in my house.'

'Don't argue with him, Jill,' Sarah said with a smile. 'You'll never win. Just accept the attention, and enjoy it while you can.'

Jill gave in, basking in the attention showered upon her. After lunch, Robert had to leave to carry on with his work, but he paused at the door of the dining-room and looked back at Jill, his face serious.

'If you have any problems at Crag House then don't forget that we're here to help you in any way,' he said.

'Problems?' Jill asked.

'We've dealt with Owen and George before,' Sarah said smoothly. 'And you're new to this way of life. What Robert means is that if you should need a couple of friends in a hurry then we're always here.'

'Thanks!' Jill smiled, but felt a shiver travel up her spine as she remembered the sinister noises in the night. 'But I'm not completely alone, you know. My father may come up from London at the week-end.'

'I'd like to meet him.' Robert spoke with hesitation. 'He's a famous author now, isn't he?'

'How do you know he's a writer?'

'Everyone round here knows about your parents!' Sarah answered. 'It's a story that could have come straight from the pages of a book.'

'It still doesn't seem real to me,' Jill admitted. 'My poor mother! She gave up everything for love only to die when I was born!'

'Your grandfather was a hard man in those days,' Robert told her. 'But the old families were always like that! I'm just glad we're living in a more easy-going time! You should come over again, Jill! I'm sorry I have to leave but I'm late for an appointment now!' He waved goodbye and left.

Jill felt a warm glow inside, and smiled when she met Sarah's gaze.

'It's great to have met you and Robert,' she said. 'I could see Crag House getting a bit lonely without other places to visit.'

'So you don't really like it there?'

'I get on well with my grandfather. It's just . . . '

'I know — Owen and George!'

'There's something else,' Jill said. 'I feel something is not quite right now they've arrived. They're obviously pretty hostile — even to each other sometimes.' She repeated the conversation she'd overheard between the two of them. 'That's why I sneaked out of the house yesterday and went for a walk on the moor.'

'That must have been awful!' Sarah was horrified. 'No wonder you're looking tired! But I know what Owen can be like. He made my life a misery the few times I went up to Crag House as a child.

'He locked me in the attic, one time, and when Robert fought Owen to let me go he ended up with a broken arm, which ended our visits.

'Owen was like a wild animal and George was always willing to follow every move he made.'

'And didn't my grandfather know anything about their behaviour?' Jill asked. 'He was under the impression they were the perfect companions for me.'

'Well, you should watch them!' Sarah's expression showed concern. 'If they feel that they should have Crag House when your grandfather dies I doubt they would let anything get in their way.'

'That's what I suspected.' Jill went on to describe the noises she had heard in the early hours, and Sarah gazed at her with growing discomfort.

'And that room next to yours is empty?' she demanded. 'To be honest, you shouldn't be staying up there with those two roaming about. I have to tell Robert about this. You should have mentioned it earlier! I'm not happy about this at all, Jill. What can I do to help? Would you like me to come and stay with you for a few days?'

'That would be lovely, but I couldn't

put you to so much trouble,' Jill replied. 'I'll be all right. I feel better for having told you.'

'Well, see how it goes. There's no reason why you should spend much of your time at the house.

'Your grandfather is an invalid, and I doubt you see him more than once a day. You could always just see him in the mornings and leave the rest of your day free.'

'That's a good idea — and it would keep me out of Owen's way!' Jill felt happier as they went out to the car, and her fears eased as they travelled through the countryside during the afternoon.

But all too soon, Sarah was driving back to Crag House and reality confronted her once more.

⋆ ⋆ ⋆

Sarah helped her into the house, where they discovered Owen standing in the hall as if he were waiting Jill's return.

The sight of his stern face sent a

shiver through Jill and her voice tremored slightly as she greeted him despite her attempt to stay calm.

'You've been gone all day!' he reproved. 'George and I have only seen you once — at breakfast.'

'I told you I prefer my own company,' Jill replied, glad that Sarah was there. 'And as I'm combining a holiday with visiting my grandfather I want to get out and see something of the places my mother knew. Apart from that, I don't really want to be tied to two strangers.'

'We wouldn't be strangers if you gave us the opportunity to get to know you,' he retorted. 'And what about Grandfather! Have you seen him at all today?'

'Yes. But he wouldn't want me to sit with him twenty-four hours a day.'

Owen started to mutter and turned on his heel to depart. Jill gazed after him with narrowed eyes, feeling the tension starting to rise.

'So that's what you're up against!' Sarah observed. 'You'll have to do something about this situation, Jill, and the sooner the better.'

'What do you suggest? I've spoken to Grandfather, and I can't harass him on the subject. I don't think he has any idea what Owen is really like.'

'In that case, why don't you tell him? You could just explain that you don't get on with Owen and if they left, your problems would be over.'

'I'll talk to Grandfather again.' Jill smiled. 'Thanks so much for helping me.'

'Well, we can help each other,' Sarah replied. 'I find life very lonely around here sometimes.'

'Thanks.' Jill glanced over her shoulder and saw George coming down the stairs. 'I'd better go and see Grandfather now! Shall I see you tomorrow?'

'Of course. I'll call about nine-thirty. But if you need to talk, call me any time.' Sarah wrote her phone number on a scrap of paper and handed it to Jill.

'Thank you.' Jill took the paper and

left it sitting on the address book on the phone table. Watching the car drive away, George spoke in Jill's ear.

'Well, you've come back to us! Have you enjoyed your day?'

'Yes, thank you!' Jill saw by his expression that he was trying hard to be pleasant. But she already knew about his brother's plan to create a good impression.

'You need to be careful not to attract the wrong kind of people,' he said. 'There are some who might try to befriend you because of your inheritance.'

'My inheritance?' Jill shook her head. 'Aren't you jumping the gun a bit? Or do you know something I don't?'

He shrugged uneasily, and she realised he was unable to strike the right note with her.

'I'd like to show you over the house,' he said. 'I've made a study of the Campbell family history, and I thought you might like to know it if you're going to remain here.'

'I'm here on a three-week holiday, George. It's been a busy year for me and all I'm concerned with is relaxing and recharging my batteries. I'm a secretary for my dad, and it's very hard work.

'Apart from that I can't walk at the moment, so looking over the house is out of the question.'

He nodded, relief showing in his face. Jill suspected that he was not too pleased with Owen's plan for him to impress her, and she watched him go back upstairs, her thoughts troubled by the situation.

But she sensed that if she maintained her independent attitude then both men would eventually get the message and leave her alone.

As she began to make her way to the stairs the doorbell rang, and Alec appeared as if from nowhere to answer it. Jill frowned, wondering if the butler had been lurking nearby in case she needed assistance against Owen.

But that was a ridiculous idea, she

thought, worrying that she was letting her imagination take control. The tensions of the situation were obviously beginning to get to her!

A woman's voice at the door caught Jill's attention and she paused, wondering who it was.

Alec showed a young woman into the hall and led her into a small room used for visitors, shielding Jill from the newcomer's gaze by carefully positioning his body. He closed the door and then turned to Jill.

'Miss Ailsa Stewart has called to introduce herself,' he said. 'Brigadier Stewart, her father, owns a nearby estate. Would you like to see her?'

'Of course I will,' Jill responded. 'Thank you, Alec.'

'I'll bring some tea, Miss Jill,' he said, and left her.

Jill found nervousness gnawing at her as she opened the door of the room, aware that Owen was spreading tension through the house. Something would have to be done to combat his plans, whatever they might be . . .

Ailsa Stewart was standing at the window, gazing out at the courtyard, and she turned immediately the door opened, smiling as she came forward with outstretched hand.

She was a tall, willowy blonde in her early twenties with an attractive face and light blue eyes.

'Hello, Jill,' she greeted warmly. 'I heard from Sarah Cameron that you had arrived so I thought I'd introduce myself. I'm Ailsa Stewart, and we're neighbours.'

'Hello, Ailsa.' Jill shook hands. 'I'm pleased to meet you! It's lovely to see another friendly face when people seem few and far between on this island. Please sit down! Alec is bringing tea. I'm still trying to adjust to life here after London!'

'Lucky you! I wish I could get to London, even just for a holiday! Are you here to stay?'

'Just for three weeks! I'm on holiday!'

'Of course. Everyone on the island

knows the story of your parents, but we didn't know of your existence, and I was surprised when Sarah called me with the news. She'd like our circle of friends to meet you.'

'She's been very kind.'

'Have you met Robert yet?'

'Yes.' Jill smiled as she remembered the first time and she explained the story very briefly to Ailsa.

'Dirk is a dear dog!' Ailsa agreed. 'And what do you think of Robert?'

'He's very nice!' A note in Ailsa's voice warned Jill to be careful talking about Robert, and she soon realised why.

'I have hopes that one day Robert and I will become more than friends! We've been going around together for years.'

Jill smiled, realising now why Ailsa had called.

Just then Alec interrupted coming in with a tray. Jill swiftly turned the conversation to other subjects, accepting the offer of a visit to Ailsa's home, before Ailsa got up to leave.

'Why don't you think about having a party? I know lots of people who could be invited,' Ailsa said. 'Everyone's wondering what it is like inside Crag House!'

'I'd love to, but Grandfather is frail and I wouldn't want to upset him.'

'I've heard he's a formidable man!' Ailsa took her leave. 'See you again. I'm sure Sarah will bring you to mine now the ice is broken. Goodbye.'

'Goodbye,' Jill replied, and watched Ailsa leave. Then she closed the heavy front door and returned to the brooding silence of the house . . .

7

Jill was expecting the time to drag, but three days passed quickly, with Sarah arriving each morning to keep her company.

She also went to the only cinema on the island with Robert before having a lovely meal with him in a restaurant. She really enjoyed the evening. Robert was great company, like Sarah, and there seemed to be a growing closeness between them.

When he took her back to Crag House she was half-expecting a good-night kiss, but it didn't come, and she wondered if Ailsa was succeeding in her quest to be more than friends with him.

The days passed easily, and Jill discovered moving around the island was no problem.

But it was when she returned to Crag

House and she was alone that life became heavy.

Owen or George were always there in the background, like a shadow, and she hated the way she always felt that someone was watching her only to discover one or the other of the brothers peering out of some doorway or other.

Owen rarely got close to her, making his hostility obvious, but George did his best to follow Owen's instructions and make friends. But Jill made no move to respond, knowing that the only reason he wanted to become friends was something to do with the inheritance.

She spent a part of each day, usually in the morning, with Hamish, sitting by his side in his room and listening to him talking of the old days, when her mother was a girl.

She noticed it was becoming easier for him to talk about her, and Jill regarded him with growing fondness.

★ ★ ★

On the Thursday evening she took a phone call from her father. She was delighted when he said he planned to travel up next day to visit for the weekend.

She made arrangements to meet him at the little port where she had landed when she had arrived, and, when she hung up and turned to go to her room, it was to find Owen standing behind her, a tense expression on his face.

His presence made Jill shiver when she realised he had been eavesdropping on her conversation with her father.

'I gather from your chat that your father is coming up to see you this weekend,' he said heavily.

'That's right!' She was amazed by his nerve, but enjoyed the fleeting expression of frustration which crossed his face at the news, and felt even happier when he spoke.

'It's a pity George and I won't be here to meet him! We have to go back to Glasgow tomorrow morning — a business problem that needs sorting out.'

Jill was astounded, but very pleased at the same time.

'That's a pity,' she responded. 'I'm sure my father would liked to have met you. Will you be coming back?'

'Certainly. I don't know when, but Grandfather wants us here so we'll be back as soon as possible.'

'And what's this business of yours?'

'We're in property, which is in a pretty bad state just now.'

Jill returned to her room feeling as if she were walking on air, and her sense of euphoria proved just how badly she was affected by Owen's presence and manner.

* * *

She slept soundly that night, and, next morning, when she broke the news of her father's visit to Hamish, he couldn't have been more pleased.

'Be there to meet him when the boat

docks,' he said. 'Buchan will drive you. I'll make sure Seward knows, and everything will be done to make your father's visit a success.'

'Thank you, Grandfather!' Jill impulsively hugged the old man.

'Owen said he and George must return to Glasgow on urgent business. It's a great pity they won't be here. But I'm pleased by this breakthrough, Jill.' His frail arms managed to return the hug.

'I'm very happy, too, Grandfather!' she replied.

When Sarah arrived that morning, Jill led her into the library, hardly able to wait to pass on the news of her father's visit. Sarah looked just as pleased.

'I'm so glad,' she said. But then her expression hardened. 'Will you tell your father about what's going on with Owen?'

'No!' Jill shook her head. 'I have thought about it, but what proof do I have? It might cause a lot of trouble if I raise any suspicions.'

'And you might let yourself in for more trouble than you can handle if you say nothing,' Sarah retorted. 'What about those strange noises you heard? From what you described I wouldn't be happy just to leave it. Did you ever manage to take a look?'

'No, but Amena did, and she said there was no sign of anything.

'I suppose it could have been my imagination — it was the first night I'd spent here, after all.'

'From the way you described it, it sounded like more than imagination!' Sarah dismissed Jill's theory with a shrug.

'I'd think very carefully about keeping quiet if I were you! Don't take any chances, Jill!'

'I'll think about it,' Jill replied uneasily.

Just then the door opened and Owen appeared. He paused in the doorway when he saw Sarah. His expression was tense and he made sure he ignored her.

'George and I are leaving now,' he

said heavily. 'But we'll be back, probably sometime later next week.' He stepped back and closed the door before Jill could reply, and Sarah gazed at her in amazement.

'They're leaving?' she demanded.

Jill explained what had happened the night before.

'Well, that says it all as far as I'm concerned,' Sarah mused. 'Owen doesn't want to meet your father, which proves he has a guilty conscience!'

'You'll come over and meet my father, won't you?' Jill asked.

'I thought you'd never ask! And Robert would certainly like to meet him. I know he's read some of your father's books!

'And he said something about getting you to procure him an autographed copy of one of them!'

Jill smiled. Excitement filled her and she could hardly sit still. Sarah noticed her obvious happiness.

'Do you have time for a trip into town?' she asked. 'I promised Robert we'd meet him for coffee at about eleven this morning. But if you have other things to do we can always postpone it.'

'Oh, no!' Jill shook her head. 'Going out somewhere should help time to pass a bit quicker. We can go now if you like.'

* * *

They drove into the nearby town, and Jill couldn't wait to see Robert again. But when it was time to meet him in a coffee shop she was surprised to see Ailsa Stewart sitting at a table with him.

She was doing most of the talking while he listened, apparently engrossed. He got up quickly when he saw Jill and Sarah coming in through the door, and introduced Ailsa.

'Jill and I have met!' Ailsa said casually. 'When Sarah told me about her I went straight to Crag House and introduced myself!'

'That was very friendly of you, Ailsa,'

Sarah observed, glancing sidelong at Jill.

'I suggested to Jill she should throw a party and invite everyone,' Ailsa said. 'It would be such fun if she could meet everyone.' She glanced at her watch.

'Is that the time? I really have to go.' She got up, smiling at Jill, then dropped a hand possessively to Robert's broad shoulder.

'I'm glad I bumped into you, Robert. I haven't seen as much of you or Sarah, as I would like. Why don't you phone me some time?'

'I will.' Robert nodded. 'I've been meaning to call at the Hall anyway. There are some business matters that I would really like to talk over with the Brigadier.'

'Then I'll tell him to expect you!'

Ailsa left the coffee shop, smiling at Jill and waving.

'Well,' Sarah observed, sitting opposite Robert so Jill could sit next to him. 'Ailsa is coming out of her shell! What brought that on, do you think? She never used to be so bold.'

'She's always had her strange moods,' Robert replied.

Jill sat down next to him, brushing his arm with her elbow, and he looked into her eyes, smiling.

'How is the ankle today?' he asked. 'Your limp seems to have cleared up a bit.'

'It's much better, thanks,' Jill replied. 'I'm hoping the next few days should clear it up.'

'Jill has some good news to tell you,' Sarah cut in.

She explained to Robert that her father had decided to visit and was arriving later on that day.

'That's wonderful,' he remarked. 'You need someone with you at the house to make sure everything is all right.'

'But you haven't heard the best of it,' Sarah continued. 'Owen overheard Jill talking on the telephone to her father about his visit, and straight away arranged for him and George to go back to Glasgow for a few days.

'Isn't that great? They left this morning while I was at Crag House. Apparently they've got some business to sort out.'

'Well, I'm glad they've gone.' Robert's face was grave as he studied Jill's relaxed expression.

'What will you tell your father about Owen and George?'

'Nothing.' Jill shook her head.

'Talk to her, will you, Robert?' Sarah interrupted. 'She won't listen to my advice.'

'I expect Jill knows what she's doing,' Robert ventured. 'But don't ever make the mistake of trusting Owen, Jill.

'I knew him very well when we were boys, and I doubt if he's changed much since those days, unless it is for the worse.'

'Are you serious?' Jill asked. She stopped talking as a waitress came for their order, and in the short silence that followed a chill crept over her which was difficult to ignore.

She recalled the strange noises she

had heard during her first night at Crag House, and the snatch of conversation she overheard between Owen and George just after their arrival.

After the waitress had taken their order, Robert covered Jill's hand with his own and leaned forward to emphasise his words.

'Knowing what I do of the Craig brothers, I wouldn't be happy to let Sarah stay under the same roof as either of them,' he said.

'And from what Sarah has told me Owen has taken your sudden appearance very badly. I wouldn't trust him any further than I could throw him! So be careful, Jill!'

'Maybe we're reading a bit too much into the situation?' Jill asked. 'I admit that I was badly frightened the other night, and, no doubt before they knew about me, Owen was under the impression that he and George would inherit Crag House and the estate.

'But would he honestly consider doing anything to remove me from

Grandfather's will?'

'It wouldn't hurt to be prepared,' Robert said, moving back when the waitress returned with their order.

Jill, looking into his face, could tell that he was quite concerned and she couldn't help feeling quite touched.

'You did say you overheard Owen telling George to make sure he got friendly with you,' Sarah reminded. 'And wasn't there talk of something happening to you if their plan didn't work?'

Jill nodded slowly, remembering the way she felt when she'd overheard that awful conversation between the two brothers.

'So your father has to be told,' Robert said firmly. 'Maybe I could talk to him and tell him what Owen is really like.

'If we came up to Crag House on Saturday I could say something to him then. I think it would be for the best, Jill!'

'Why don't you both come for tea

then?' Jill asked.

'We'd love to,' Sarah said. 'Wouldn't we, Robert?'

'I'll look forward to it,' he replied, and Jill realised that he was still covering her hand with his.

'I'd love to speak to your father about his books.'

'So that's settled!' Sarah smiled. 'What time would you like us?'

'How about four? But I'm not so sure we should say anything to Father about Owen and George.

'I know my father! He'd take the bull by the horns and there could be a lot of trouble! I have Grandfather to think of, too! I can't afford to upset him, not when he's poorly. I would hate for any of this trouble to get back to him — there's no knowing how the shock would affect him and I don't really want to be the one responsible for upsetting him in any way.'

'Your grandfather should know what kind of men Owen and George are!' Sarah told her.

'You've got to get this situation into perspective, Jill! You overheard Owen ordering George to make up to you, as they planned, and if that doesn't work they would want something to happen to you!

'Well, what exactly does that mean to you?' Sarah went on, obviously quite upset by the whole business.

'Think about it. And in the meantime I'll tell you what it means to me! You could suddenly find yourself in a lot of trouble when you least expect it!'

Jill nodded, a shiver travelling through her body. She knew Sarah was talking sense but were Owen and George really prepared to be so calculating?

Sarah's stark words were sinking in, and tension held her in its frightening grip, having already subdued her excitement at her father's visit.

So where would it all end? She shook her head. Only time would tell . . .

8

Later that afternoon, when the small passenger boat from the mainland tied up at the quay, Jill could hardly contain her excitement and anxiously searched the faces of the passengers standing on the deck.

At last she saw her father and waved, and the sight of his smiling face chased the last shreds of worry from her mind.

He was carrying a small case and had his familiar, brown raincoat slung over his arm, and Jill threw herself into his arms.

'Dad, I'm so pleased to see you!' she cried, hugging him tightly. 'I can't believe you're actually here at last!'

'Hey, steady on!' He staggered under the weight of her greeting. 'Anyone would think we haven't seen each other for years!'

'That's what it feels like to me,' she

responded, stepping back to look at him. 'Oh, Dad, I'm so pleased you were able to come!'

'You sound very relieved that I'm here.' His eyes narrowed as he looked at her.

'Has your grandfather been giving you any trouble?'

'No!' She shook her head. 'He's been so sweet! I've really taken to him, Dad, and I wish I had met him years ago.'

'Well, I'm glad about that! So if it isn't your grandfather then who has been upsetting you? You seem very tense — not yourself at all.'

He studied her face, and Jill drew a deep breath, reluctant to give anything away which might worry her father. She hoped her tense mood at that moment wasn't too apparent to him.

'It's nothing really, Dad! Crag House just takes a bit of getting used to. I think it got to me when I arrived. Especially knowing that Mother lived here as a girl! I'm sure I can sense her sometimes!'

She led him to the car, limping slightly.

'What have you been doing to yourself since I saw you last?' he demanded. 'You're limping.'

'I'll tell you all about it on the way to Crag House.' She smiled at the memory of her first meeting with Robert.

'You'll be pleased to know I have made a couple of good friends here. They live quite close by to the house.' She introduced Buchan, who stowed her father's case in the boot of the car.

'There's so much to tell you, Dad! And I really hope you'll be able to feel relaxed here.

'I remember you telling me about the last time you saw Crag House, when Mother left with you, and I'm sure you must have some ghosts to lay now you're back!'

'You're right!' He sighed. 'I haven't stopped thinking about it since I agreed to visit.

'Yesterday I was quite prepared to call it off, but I always knew it was

132

something I'd have to do sooner or later.' He smiled at her and patted her arm as Buchan drove from the town. 'Now tell me what's been happening since your arrival.'

★　★　★

Jill talked all the way to Crag House, avoiding the strange goings-on, although she explained about Owen and George.

When the car drew up in the courtyard Jill kept quiet as her father got out and took his time looking around, for she could guess at the nature of his thoughts. After a short while he looked at her, a half-smile on his face.

'I never thought I'd see this place again!' he remarked.

'I hope it doesn't hurt too much,' she replied. 'You must have some very bitter memories, Dad, and especially about Grandfather!'

'Events have gone full circle, Jill!' He sighed and took her arm to lead her up the steps to the front door, which was opened for them by Alec.

The old butler was smiling, and Jill's father left her side to run up the remaining steps to grasp Alec's hand.

Jill felt a surge of emotion as she watched.

Alec was delighted to see her father, and, when Amena stepped into the doorway to get her first glimpse of the man who had taken her mistress away so many years before, tears welled up in Jill's eyes.

They finally managed to cross the threshold, and Jill could see pleasure on the faces of both Amena and Alec.

'The master would like to see you immediately,' Alec said. 'Shall I show you straight up to his room?'

'Please do!' Jim Telford glanced at Jill. 'Perhaps I'd better see Hamish alone this first time.'

'Of course.' Jill nodded. 'I'm in Mother's old room, and Amena has put you in next to me. We'll take your case up just now.'

He nodded and followed Alec while Jill walked with Amena to her father's room.

They entered, and Jill looked around, wondering about the noises that had seemed to emanate from this spot.

She gazed at the featureless wall, recalling the sounds, and suppressed a shiver as foreboding touched her mind.

But then, remembering that Owen and George had been called away, she felt happier.

She dragged herself from her thoughts, aware that Amena had spoken, and turned to face the old housekeeper.

'I'm sorry, I didn't hear what you said,' she apologised.

'No need for apologies, lassie,' Amena replied. 'I know exactly what's going through your mind. We're all touched by this reunion, I can tell you.'

'I wish my mother could see us all here together.' Jill sighed.

'I'll go and put the kettle on,' Amena countered. 'I think we could all do with a nice cup of tea!'

'I'll bring Dad to the kitchen when he's finished seeing Grandfather,' Jill said.

Left alone, Jill looked around the room again, and suddenly felt that somehow she was being watched.

She frowned and walked to the door, filled with tension, the silence grating at every nerve.

Was Crag House haunted? Did the spirit of her own mother wander this ancestral home in torment for her lost life and love?

Jill drew a deep breath and held it for some moments, trying to control her feelings.

She could hear the rapid beating of her heart and was aware of the pounding of blood at her temples. Then she exhaled and felt some of the tension lift.

She felt utterly drained, but knowing her father was here gave her a sense of security — she only wished he could stay a bit longer.

But the future would have to take care of itself, she realised, because there was nothing she could do about it herself . . .

* * *

Jill waited for what seemed an eternity before her father emerged from Hamish's room.

When she saw his face she realised just how traumatic this visit was for him. He had lived for many years without the moral support of his wife's family, and now, it seemed, the breach was healed.

'Let's go down to the kitchen, Dad,' she said. 'Amena is making tea!'

'That sounds lovely.' He grasped Jill's hand as they descended the stairs. 'I'm so glad I came! Hamish is older than I thought he would be — and it's time matters were put right between us.

'I used to blame him for your mother's death, but of course I was wrong, and Hamish also knows that his attitude all those years ago was wrong. Unfortunately, it's too late for either of us to make a difference now, but you'll be able to, Jill.'

'I don't understand!' Jill frowned.

'It's quite simple, really. Hamish told me that you will inherit the estate when the time comes, and it's going to change your life.

'If you had been brought up knowing about your inheritance you would have been used to the idea by now.

'But even though you've only just learned about it I still think you'll make some wise decisions.'

'But I don't have to make any just yet,' Jill replied. 'Let's forget all that now, Dad. I want to enjoy this week-end! I'm not really concerned with what I may or may not inherit.

'I'm just sorry that it isn't going to the person who really deserved it — and that's Mother.'

He nodded, his pale eyes reflecting his feelings, and Jill squeezed his hand. It was wonderful to have him here, to know that at last any nagging doubts he had harboured over the years were at last being laid to rest.

But she was aware that the week-end would flash by, and dreaded the thought of his departure . . .

After a reviving cup of tea, Jim Telford wanted to look around the estate and revisit the spots he had last seen in the company of his beloved wife. Jill enjoyed the afternoon, too, but it was difficult not to get emotional — a lot of the places had been so personal to her parents.

But she realised this was a phase she had to pass through, and when it was over she would be able to settle down, albeit to a totally different way of life to the one she thought she would be facing . . .

* * *

On Saturday morning, Jim wanted to travel farther afield, to revisit some of the places on the island that held special significance for him, and Jill was happy to go with him.

'We'll have to be back before four this afternoon,' she told him. 'I've asked Sarah and Robert to have tea with us.

'They've become very good friends, Dad, and are dying to meet you. Robert has read some of your books, and I'm sure he'd like an autographed copy of one of them.'

'I'm looking forward to meeting them,' he replied with a smile, and Jill hugged him, wishing their week-end together could last for ever.

The morning flew by, and, as they were returning to Crag House, Jill decided to talk to him about what was worrying her.

She could see Crag House in the distance, towering above the surrounding countryside, and a pang of fear made her shiver as she thought about staying on after her father's departure.

'Do you have to return to London tomorrow, Dad?' she asked.

'I'm afraid so!' He shook his head. 'I

really shouldn't have taken the time to visit at all this week-end.

'I have a meeting in London on Monday morning with my agent, and after lunch there's an appointment with my publisher. We're angling for a new series, so it is important to tie things up as soon as possible. It's such a competitive business these days, Jill.'

'I shall miss you!' she responded. 'I could do with some support here until I get used to the place and the idea that it'll all be mine soon.'

'I can imagine how you feel, and I'm sorry I don't have the time to stay on. But how about if I try to sort out my business as quickly as I can and then come back here? Would that make you feel better?'

'Thanks, Dad!' She smiled. 'But what about after I inherit, what then? Will you move up here with me? I don't think I could stay on here alone.'

'I understand. I know we have a lot to talk about and I promise I'll come back as soon as I can and we'll try to sort it all out.'

Jill squeezed his arm, content that they would work out a solution to what seemed impossible problems.

★ ★ ★

That afternoon when Sarah and Robert arrived, Jill was delighted with their enthusiasm at meeting her father.

He and Robert hit it off immediately and Robert wanted to know all about his writing career. He told Jill's father he had always wanted to write and had once or twice attempted some short stories. But running his own business took up all of his time.

Jim loved to talk about his work and no matter how often he was asked about it, he never seemed to tire of the subject that was closest to his heart, apart from Jill.

'You should let Jill see some of your short stories,' Jim said. 'She always edits my work and always seems to know just what is needed. If she likes it she can forward it to me and I'll give you an opinion.

'But there is no secret to success apart from determination. And of course, a little bit of talent helps, too!'

'Thanks for your advice.' Robert's eyes gleamed. 'I might just take you up on your offer.'

'Oh, dear!' Sarah whispered to Jill. 'Once Robert gets on the subject of writing he can become quite a bore! He hasn't been able to concentrate on anything since we told him your father was visiting!'

Jill smiled. It was such a help to her — having friends such as Sarah and Robert.

'Not to worry,' she replied. 'Dad will never get bored as long as he's talking about writing.'

After tea, Jim and Robert went for a stroll in the gardens. Jill watched them from where she sat by a window.

They were talking very seriously and at great length as they walked to and fro among the flower beds. Sarah, chatting to Jill about her day, glanced from the window and smiled as she watched the two men.

'Robert couldn't be happier. He drives me to distraction sometimes, talking about writing. It's not something I've really thought about myself — what about you, Jill?'

'I've never really had the time.' Jill shook her head. 'For as long as I can remember I've always read Father's work, and trained for the day when I could become his secretary.'

'Have you told your father about Owen and George?' Sarah asked quietly.

'No. I've thought about it. But he's too busy to spare any time to stay on here so I'll have to cope on my own.

'But if I'm lucky, Owen and George won't return too soon. Hopefully their business will keep them there and Father might already be back before they have the chance to show up again.'

'Remember, don't under-estimate

Owen,' Sarah warned. 'If he's determined to get a share of this estate then you could be heading for trouble, Jill!'

'I'd already thought about that. But what can I do without proof?'

⋆   ⋆   ⋆

Jill was thoughtful during the rest of the evening, and, after Sarah and Robert had departed, Jim smiled at her and sat down.

'I'm glad they came round,' he said. 'They're both very nice, Jill, just the kind of people you need to get to know.

'You've never really had the chance to make real friends working for me — it can be quite an isolating way of life. It's all right for me to be dedicated and spend all hours writing. But I realise I've been pushing you quite hard these past few years.'

'I've enjoyed every moment of it,' she responded. 'I wouldn't change my work for anything!'

He smiled.

'I think it's time I started looking for a new secretary,' he admitted. 'You have enough on your plate now without trying to take care of me.'

'Well, my twenty-first birthday certainly brought some changes. I can't believe all this is really happening. I'm going to miss you when you leave tomorrow, you know.'

'I'll come back as soon as I can,' he promised. 'And I'll spend a week or two here on holiday.

'Now I've broken the ice with your grandfather I have to think about your future and what I can do to make it easier for you.'

'Are you talking about moving up here with me?' She was unable to hide her pleasure at his words.

'Why not?' He shrugged. 'If you can sacrifice your way of life in order to inherit what was your mother's then it's the least I can do in return. After all, I still feel responsible for you and I'm sure the atmosphere up here would be great for my work!'

'If only you could!' Jill's eyes gleamed. 'There wouldn't be any problems then.'

'Leave it to me!' He patted her arm, then stifled a yawn. 'I think it's time to turn in,' he said. 'I have to be away early in the morning.'

'I'm going to miss you, Dad,' she said softly.

'Cheer up! It won't be for long!' he replied.

Jill was not so sure, and lay brooding when she went to bed, lying in the darkness, her ears strained for the slightest suspicious sound although she was comforted by the knowledge that her father was in the next room. But tomorrow he would be gone, and that stark knowledge frightened her . . .

9

Jill was filled with mixed feelings as she watched her father board the little boat on the start of his trip back to London. He waved to her from the deck as the craft left its mooring at the stone quay, and she waved back until the vessel had almost passed from sight.

Then she went back to Crag House, aware of all the fears that had filled her mind before her father's arrival.

But at least Owen and George hadn't come back yet, and that was something to be thankful for.

Buchan drove the big car along the narrow roads, and Jill watched the countryside flashing by, her thoughts intent on the previous day, when Sarah and Robert had met her father.

She could feel a warmth spread through her as she thought of Robert. There was something so dependable about him, and having him around helped her a lot. Then she thought of Ailsa Stewart and a frown touched her smooth forehead.

Sarah was already waiting at Crag House when Jill returned, and taking one look at Jill's expression, she threw an arm around her shoulder.

'Why don't you come and stay with us for a day or two?' she asked. 'I know for a fact that Robert would love to show you around the farm.'

'I'd better look in on Grandfather before I make any plans,' Jill replied.

Sarah nodded, and Jill went along to Hamish's room, arriving at the door just as Amena emerged. The housekeeper closed the door and took Jill's arm, leading her a few paces along the corridor.

'Your grandfather is not well this morning, Jill,' Amena said. 'I've sent for the doctor and he'll be here soon.'

'Is he going to be all right?' Jill shook her head. 'What can we do?'

'Nothing, I'm afraid. He's really very

tired after the excitement of the last few days. But your father had to come and see Hamish. There was no other way of resolving the situation. And it was a good meeting between them. Hamish needed to get it behind him.'

'Can I go in and see him?'

'Of course. He's already been asking for you.'

Jill went into the room. The curtains were open and light was flooding in. Hamish lay motionless in the bed, his eyes closed, and Jill was quite alarmed at the sight of his pallid features.

As she moved towards him, Hamish opened his eyes, and a smile touched his lips when he saw her.

'Your father is on his way home then,' he said.

'Yes, Grandfather. He had to get home to see to some business. But he was very happy to see you.'

'I was pleased he came.' The old man sighed deeply. 'And before I forget, I want to tell you that a lot of your mother's belongings are in the attic.

When she left with your father that last time I had everything she didn't take put into trunks and stored in the attic, where they've always been.

'They're yours now, lassie, to do with what you will. Don't worry about me! It's only old age affecting me. I'll be back to normal in a day or so. Then I'll need to talk to you about your future.' He fell silent and closed his eyes, and moments later Jill heard him snoring gently.

She tiptoed silently from the room. It would be dreadful if something happened to Hamish before she had the chance to really get to know him. He had spent years alone in this big house with nothing but memories to keep him company, and now just as she had arrived to alleviate his pain he seemed in danger of slipping away . . .

'How is he?' Sarah asked, when Jill joined her friend in the library.

'I think he got very excited at seeing my father again. I do hope he'll be all right. I think I should stay here, Sarah, at least until the doctor has been.'

'Of course. You should be all right while Owen and George are away.' Sarah rose to leave. 'Keep in touch, Jill, and if you're worried about anything then just pick up the telephone and call me.'

Jill nodded and Sarah left. When she was alone at last she sighed deeply and went along to the kitchen to talk to Amena.

The housekeeper was busy with her morning chores, and Jill needed reassurance about Hamish.

'He's very often like this,' Amena said, 'so try not to worry. He has a strong spirit and I'm sure knowing that you're here will keep him going.'

Jill went to the library and read until Doctor Galloway arrived.

'And how is your ankle this morning, Miss Telford?' he asked.

'Much better, thank you, Doctor! But I'm worried about my grandfather!'

'Och, well, he's an old man! You have to expect these ups and downs. He does well for his age! What you must do is keep him from getting excited.'

'Yes. Well, he had a busy time over the week-end!' Jill explained about her father's visit as she took him to Hamish's room. 'It seemed to go very well, considering, but it's obviously taken its toll.'

Hamish woke up when they entered the room and chatted easily with the doctor, who checked his pulse and listened to his heart with a stethoscope.

'I expect you'll outlive me,' he announced with a smile. 'Just rest for a few days and you'll be all right.'

'You don't need to tell me that,' Hamish retorted. 'It's that housekeeper of mine who's the trouble. She sends for you if the wind blows on me! Next time she calls, ignore her!'

'Ay, well, I don't mind visiting you for a wee while now and again! I like to keep an eye on my older patients. And you'll be all right so long as you don't burn the candle at both ends.' The doctor laughed, and Jill accompanied him to the front door.

'It's as I've said,' he told her. 'Too much excitement is bad for him. But I'm sure he knows that himself and won't overdo it.'

'Thank you, Doctor.' Jill sighed with relief as she closed the door. She stood for a moment in the silence of the hall, then decided it was time to have a look in the attic.

There was a door at the top of the stairs which opened as she pushed it. She paused to peer into the darkness, feeling nervous and knowing that the slightest sound would have her scurrying back to the ground floor. But she was gripped by an overwhelming desire to see what her mother had left behind all those years before.

She fumbled just inside the doorway, found a light switch and flicked it. Relief filled her as light flooded the room she found herself in. All around were innumerable crates, boxes and jumbled, unwanted items lying around the sides.

The attic was surprisingly clean, and she went in leaving the door open. She decided to search through the nearest crate.

When she found a thick diary lying on top of a pile of folded clothes she snatched it up eagerly and opened it, delighted when she saw her mother's name pencilled on the first page.

Her mother's last diary! She turned the thin pages, noting the neat handwriting, and her eyes blurred when she found the last entry and read the simple sentences.

I am leaving home today! Father won't see me off! He has disowned me! But I would rather forego everything here than lose Jim. He is the light of my life and we will make a home in London.

Perhaps time will ease the pain Father feels, and I shall live in the hope that he will forgive me! Goodbye, dear house, and all that I love! A greater love calls me but I will never forget my home and all it has meant to me!

A tear landed on the page and Jill

realised she was crying. She put the book aside, sobbing loudly as she grieved for the woman who had given birth to her before losing that dream of happiness for which she had sacrificed everything.

Fate had been so cruel to her and now, more than twenty years later, the sad record of her uncertainty and mental torture was revealed to the only monument she had left on earth to mark her existence — and that was Jill!

She dried her eyes, glad that finally she had been able to let go some of the emotion that had been building up inside. She sighed and read on, reliving her mother's hopes and fears with the hurtful knowledge that soon after the diary had been written, her mother had met her untimely end giving birth to her only child.

* * *

Jill lost all track of time as she read the diary, her mother's heartache and worry coming clearly through the simple sentences. Then a terrific crash startled her and she sprang up, frightened out of her wits, to discover that the attic door had slammed shut.

With her heart racing, she ran to the door and turned the handle, tugging with all her strength. But it would not open.

Her hands hurt with the effort of pulling the door, but nothing would budge it. Finally, she fell back a step and stared at the door, breathless, then renewed her attack, hammering and calling for help until she sank to her knees in frustration, resting her head against the solid wood panels.

Silence closed in and a sense of eerie fear enveloped her. She looked around the massive room, her throat tightening as her nerve wavered.

Then making an effort to regain control, she stood up to take stock of the situation, wondering how the door had become jammed.

There was no key in the lock when

she'd gone in but peering at the door she could now see that the lock had been turned.

There was a window in the sloping roof, but Jill could see no sign of the ground when she looked through it, only a jumble of dull slates. The window was jammed shut, and too small for her to crawl through had she been able to open it.

She returned to the door, thoroughly alarmed now, and picked up a thick piece of wood in the hope she could smash through the panels. But she had no luck. Sitting down to think about it, she remained motionless until a voice called to her from outside.

'Miss Jill, are you all right in there?' It was Alec, and his voice came faintly through the thick panels.

'Alec, the door slammed shut. I think it's locked but there's no key!'

'Give me a few moments! I'll get a key from Amena!'

Jill relaxed, but it seemed to be ages before a key clicked into the lock and the door was opened. Alec confronted her, frowning.

'Did you have a key?' he demanded.

'No! The door wasn't locked.' She explained what she was doing in the attic. 'The door suddenly slammed, and I could see it was locked.'

'You're right,' he agreed. 'I had to unlock it. But the only keys are kept in the kitchen. And we don't lock this door, anyway!'

'Well, it couldn't lock itself.' she insisted. 'And why did it slam with such force? There's no draught on the stairs!'

'Maybe the force of it slamming sprung the lock! But I have no idea what made it slam. It's a good job I was looking for you. Robert Cameron had phoned to speak to you and when I couldn't find you downstairs or in your room I told him I'd get you to call him back!'

'Thank you!' Jill suppressed a sigh. She felt shaky from the incident, and her knees were weak as she followed Alec down to the ground floor. Straight away she phoned Robert, and when she heard the sound of his voice she felt like crying.

'Hello,' he greeted. 'Sarah told me about your grandfather not being well. Has the doctor been yet?'

'Yes. Hamish should be all right if he rests.'

'So what are you doing today? Sarah said she invited you to spend it with us but I have a better idea. Why don't I come and pick you up and we'll drive somewhere.

'We could have dinner out, and it would give me the chance to talk to you about your father and to let you see some of my stories.'

'I'd like that.' Jill spoke almost without thinking. At the moment she was consumed by an overwhelming need to get away from Crag House.

'Fine. I'll call for you in about twenty minutes.'

'I'll be ready and waiting,' she replied.

She went to the kitchen to tell Amena

her plans then sat in the library until Alec came with the message that Robert had arrived. Jill hurried to the door, and almost fell into Robert's arms.

He led her to his car and settled her in the front passenger seat, before pausing to look at her.

'What's wrong?' he asked. 'You look really upset.'

'I had a fright, that's all. It was nothing really, but at the time it was quite scary.'

He got into the car and turned to face her, his expression grave.

'Why don't you tell me about it,' he encouraged.

Jill explained, and watched his expression change. He shook his head, then busied himself with driving away from the house. When they were out on the main road he broke the silence.

'I told your father what I think of Owen,' he said, 'and he agreed that you shouldn't take any chances. I think you should do as Sarah suggests and come and stay with us for a few days.'

'It's very good of you,' Jill admitted. 'But I have to get used to Crag House at some time, and if I leave now, then I'll never find the nerve to return. Owen and George aren't here now so nothing can happen.'

'What about that attic door? It didn't just lock itself.' Robert's tone was grim. 'I'm afraid I don't believe that the lock sprung itself when the door slammed. And what made the door slam? You said there was no draught, and how long were you in the attic before it actually happened?'

'About an hour!' Jill shrugged.

'Well, it would have slammed long before then if a draught had caused it.'

'It's beyond me.' She sighed. 'And I'd like to forget it now.'

'You can't just forget it!' he insisted. 'Don't you want to get to the bottom of it? Who else was in the house?'

'Grandfather, Alec and Amena!' Jill didn't like the line her thoughts were taking. 'Please stop talking about it now!' she begged. 'I need to think about it for myself to try to make sense of it.'

Robert nodded, and there was silence while he drove along the winding road that crossed the moor.

Jill felt more relaxed the farther they drew away from Crag House, and when Robert finally parked on a cliff overlooking a small cove she had almost recovered her feeling of control.

She looked at Robert, envying him his uncomplicated life, and suppressed a shudder as she imagined returning to Crag House to spend a lonely night within its frightening confines. Even the thought of her mother's courage could not outweigh her fears.

But throughout the day she recovered her nerve and began to enjoy herself. Robert was good company and she knew she was attracted to him. He was attentive without crowding her, and when they stopped at an inn for lunch she was beginning to wish the day would never end.

By the afternoon she felt relaxed and

far more her usual self, and Robert kept up his cheerful conversation as he drove back along the coast before cutting inland towards his farm.

'Maybe we could do this more often, Jill,' he said eventually. 'I work too hard and long, you know! Sarah is always telling me I should take more time for myself and I'd really like to spend more time with you — if you want to, of course.'

Jill looked at him. 'That would be really nice, but I have a feeling Ailsa wouldn't be too happy about it!'

'Ailsa!' He frowned, then smiled. 'Ah, Ailsa! Well, I'm not sure what she's got in mind, but I've always just seen her as a friend. We've known each other for years because we're neighbours, although she was always Sarah's friend rather than mine. To tell you the truth, she's not really my type.'

'I've got a feeling she feels differently,' Jill said. 'When she came round to see me I think she was warning me off you!'

'Really!' He glanced at her, his eyes narrowing. 'I suppose she can be a bit possessive but she's never actually said anything to me about getting involved with each other. Maybe she's reading far too much into our friendship.'

'Well, whatever she thinks, I don't want to be the one to tread on her toes. I don't need any more enemies around here.'

'Why don't you stay with us for a few days?' he asked as the farm came into sight.

'I'd love to, but I have to think about Grandfather!' She spoke slowly, aware that she had no real choice but to think about him. She had come to Crag House to visit Hamish and couldn't just abandon him.

'It can't be easy for you.' Robert spoke with great feeling, and pulled the car over to the verge and stopped. 'These should be the happiest days of your life, coming back to your mother's old home, meeting your grandfather for the first time. But it hasn't quite worked out for you and I can tell you're really worried!'

He reached out and took her hand in his, his face filled with concern, and Jill experienced something she'd never felt before.

Suddenly needing comfort and someone to hold on to she couldn't help but reach out for him. Then she was in his arms and his strength surrounded her, filling her with a warmth that washed away her fears instantly.

She had hated being alone at Crag House, but now she sensed that Robert would stand by her, look after her, and she closed her eyes and gave herself up to his power.

The next moment his lips were against hers and she was filled with a wonderful sensation. He kissed her, gently at first, then with growing passion, and she responded with all the fire that was in her, finding, for the first time since meeting Owen and George Craig, that they no longer had the power to frighten her . . .

10

It was almost dark when Jill finally tore herself from the dream into which she had fallen and pushed herself away from Robert, allowing reality to return to her dazed mind. Her face was flushed and her eyes were bright with happiness as she looked at Robert.

'Are you sure you won't stay at the farm, Jill?' Robert asked, his eyes pleading. 'You look so much more relaxed than you did this morning and I'm sure getting away from Crag House for a while would do you the world of good. You never see your grandfather at night, and if you want, I could drive you back to Crag House first thing every morning, before anyone is awake.'

'I'd like to, but supposing something happens to Grandfather in the night and Alec can't find me?'

'Take him into your confidence. You

167

could tell them what your plans are. He and Amena are on your side and they never liked Owen and George.' He laughed. 'I've never met anyone who did like those two!'

'I'll think about it,' Jill promised. 'There won't be any problems while Owen and George are away, but when they call back I'll definitely think about it.'

'Fine. I feel much better now. But we'll check at Crag House when I take you home, just in case they're due back, and if they are back then I won't let you stay in the house.'

Jill nodded, comforted by his assurance.

'Thank you, Robert,' she said quietly. 'Now I'll have to go home!' She suppressed a shiver as she pictured Crag House, and the growing darkness outside the car seemed to take on a sense of hostility. 'Dad must be back in London now. He's probably trying to get in touch with me.'

Robert started the car, and Jill

couldn't stop thinking about what had happened between them on the way back to the house.

She'd been attracted to him from the moment they'd met but hadn't imagined he'd felt the same for her.

He seemed to draw her so strongly she began to wish he would stop the car and take her into his arms again.

When the dark shadow of Crag House loomed up before them, tension began to overwhelm her. Robert stopped the car in the courtyard, where a light threw a shaft of brilliance over the steps and entrance. Suppressing a shiver, Jill got out of the car.

Returning here under such pressure gave her the feeling that Crag House itself was hostile to her, and she thought of her mother in an attempt to summon up strength to go back in.

Alec was there to open the door and Robert followed Jill inside. She looked around the dimly lit hall and any nerve she had faded away. She felt so small and the house so threatening.

'I'm glad I've caught you, Mr Robert,' Alec said. 'Miss Sarah called and left the message that you are to ring her immediately you arrived.'

'Thank you!' Robert frowned as he caught Jill's worried gaze. 'Excuse me.' He went to the telephone and dialled a number, while Jill watched him intently.

'Hello, Sarah,' he said eventually. 'Has something happened?' He listened for some moments, and Jill saw a frown appear on his face and remain there until he hung up and turned. Then he forced a smile and shook his head.

'No problems,' he said. 'Your father called Sarah after he had rung you here and failed to get you, and she just wanted you to know that he is safely back in London.'

'Yes, he phoned earlier,' Alec said. 'He won't be at home now. He had some business to attend to this afternoon.'

'Thank you, Alec. I know Dad has a busy day tomorrow. I'll try to get hold of him in the morning before he leaves for his appointments.'

She pictured their neat little house in London and, for a moment, wished she was there, back in the old routine that had made her life so comfortable.

But knowing she might never return to that suddenly struck her and she wondered what she was doing here in a strange, dark, old house that really had no part of her.

Then she looked at Robert, seeing concern in his eyes, and drew a deep breath as she cut off the stream of fearful thoughts and steeled herself.

It was silly to think negatively, she told herself firmly. Life had moved on from all those familiar things back in London. She was no longer the same person who had flown north in such excitement.

And there was Robert to think of now, for he had suddenly loomed large in her life, and she knew that if she returned to London right there and then she would miss him, and would probably want to return to Crag House even with all the worry it contained.

'Thank you, Robert, for a lovely time,' she said, and he reached out and grasped her hand. But she looked at Alec, who was waiting patiently in the background. 'Has there been any word about Owen and George returning?'

'Not a word, miss. And your grandfather is better than he was this morning. He looks more rested this evening, and by tomorrow I'm sure he'll be his old self again. Is there anything I can get you just now?'

'No thank you, Alec. I'm sorry we've disturbed your evening. Mr Robert will be leaving shortly, and I'll lock up after he has left.'

'Thank you, miss.' Alec departed soundlessly.

Jill looked at Robert.

'I hoped you wouldn't be leaving just yet!'

He looked over his shoulder, saw that Alec was now out of earshot, and grasped her hand.

'I'm not leaving at all,' he replied.

Jill caught her breath.

'What do you mean?' she demanded.

He shook his head.

'I really don't know what to make of it,' he said slowly. 'That's why I'm not going to take any chances!

'Sarah said she was out riding late this afternoon, and when she passed a derelict cottage on the edge of your estate she caught a glimpse of someone acting quite suspiciously.

'She wanted to find out more so she left her horse and sneaked back to check and saw Owen and George in the cottage. She overheard some of their conversation and discovered that they were waiting for darkness so they could sneak into Crag House!'

Jill froze at his words and fear crept over her. She reached out to Robert and he drew her into the comfort of his arms, holding her close.

'This is much more serious than anyone thinks, Jill! I know Owen better than most, from the early days in this house, which is why I talked very seriously to your father on Saturday about what you'd said about noises here in the night.

'Fortunately, your father agreed with me, and he didn't get off the boat when he reached the mainland and made the return trip this afternoon. We arranged for Sarah to pick him up and take him to the farm.'

Jill felt as if she had slipped into a nightmare.

'Dad didn't return to London!' She gasped. 'So that means Sarah's message wasn't true! Where's Dad now?'

'That's what I'm wondering, and why I'm telling you this now!' Robert's tone was grave. 'Years ago, your father discovered a secret entrance to the house which he used to see your mother against your grandfather's wishes, and found out that the house is honeycombed with secret passages.

'He was going to use the entrance to come into the house tonight to watch over you.

'He cancelled all his appointments in

London, meaning to stay under cover in this house each night and sleep at the farm each day until he could satisfy himself that you were in no danger.'

'I can hardly believe this!' Jill gasped. 'And is he in the house now?'

'He is! But Sarah found out about Owen and George after she had dropped your father nearby so she couldn't tell him they were back.'

'Then we'd better call the police! It'd be awful if Father ran into Owen and George not knowing they were here.'

'I suggested to your father on Saturday that the police should be told but he didn't want that. He wanted to check this out for himself. Now he's somewhere in the house, and could be at the mercy of your cousins.'

Jill squeezed Robert's hand, her mind swimming with fear.

'I think we should call the police and have them search the house,' she said firmly. 'I don't want to take any risks if Owen and George are up to no good.'

'They must have something in mind,

sneaking back to the island when they are supposed to be in Glasgow!' Robert paused as a thought struck him, then added, 'That's if they ever left! If they didn't go to Glasgow, then maybe they were behind you getting shut in the attic!'

Jill caught her breath at the implication of his words and shivered.

'Did Father tell you where this secret entrance is?' she demanded.

'I'm afraid he didn't! Maybe we should take Alec into our confidence and see if he can tell us anything. I'm sure if anyone knows about that sort of thing then he will!'

'I've often felt I was being secretly watched in some of the rooms here!' Jill shook her head as she remembered. 'And those noises coming from a locked room! If there are secret passages then that's how they were made! Owen must have known about the passages and is using them now!' The knowledge frightened her. 'What can we do, Robert?'

'We can check for ourselves! If there are secret passages the walls will have to be at least three feet thick. Let's go up to your room and find out.'

Jill led the way, eager to know what was going on. She could hardly believe that her father was here instead of in London! And all this intrigue going on behind her back! What on earth was happening?

She led the way into her room and waited for Robert to follow her, clenching her hands as she watched him examine the walls, running his hands over the smooth expanses and pressing the skirting boards and picture rails.

'I've seen secret passages in a lot of old houses that were built in Scotland in the eighteenth century,' Robert informed her. 'There was a lot of mystery in those days. The English were enemies, and terrible battles were fought.'

He broke off when his fingers located a sliding panel which creaked open to reveal a cavity the size of a door.

'There you are!' he said, smiling

grimly. 'The dark side of Crag House!'

Jill stared at the cavity, stunned by the sight of it, aware that locking the door of the room when she heard those strange noises had offered no protection whatever! All she had done was lock herself in with the menace!

Horror filled her and she felt vulnerable despite Robert being there. But worry for her father filled her, and she resolutely went to Robert's side to peer into the narrow passage that was dusty and liberally strewn with cobwebs.

'Look! Footprints, Jill!' Robert pointed to the tell-tale marks in thick dust that had accumulated over two centuries. 'Whatever made those noises must be human!'

Jill felt stifled as she gazed at the significant marks. Owen and George had been skulking around the house like two animals! She had no idea what it all meant, but it was obvious that something quite serious was happening, and she was thankful Robert was at her side.

'What can we do?' she demanded.

'We need a light! Do you have a torch in the room?'

'No. I could ask Alec for one.'

'Please! But don't say anything about this. If we can we'll find your father, and leave decisions up to him. But he must be told about Owen and George.'

Jill hurried down to Alec's quarters, where the butler and his wife were watching TV.

Armed with a powerful torch, she returned to her room, but stopped when she realised Robert had disappeared. The cavity was gaping blackly, sinister and frightening, but she overcame her fear, desperate to find Robert. Maybe he had stepped into the passage to check it out.

She switched on the torch, and entered the cavity, dispelling the darkness inside with the powerful beam. She caught a movement in the shadows and started nervously. Then her heart seemed to miss a beat as a hand darted out of the shadows and grasped her wrist . . .

179

11

Jill stared in horror when George Craig stepped out of the cavity, holding her wrist in a vice-like grip. His face was set in a grim expression, his eyes bright and glassy, as if he was in some kind of trance.

'Come with me!' he rapped, and dragged Jill into the cavity.

'Where's Robert?' she gasped, struggling to break his grip on her wrist.

'Owen's taking care of him! Come on. I'll take you to him.'

Jill stopped struggling and George walked along the passage, the powerful torch in his free hand throwing a brilliant glare over the rough, stone walls surrounding them. Jill was stunned by the swift turn of events, and shock almost blanked out her thoughts. She clung to her torch mindlessly, unaware that it had been switched off in her struggle with George.

'What are you going to do with us?' she demanded tremulously. 'You must know you can't get away with this, George.'

'Owen thinks we can! It's your fault, anyway. I thought you and I could have married eventually and then none of this would have been necessary. But we're not going to lose the estate just because you've turned up at the last minute! We've got something planned for you that will be the end of the matter.'

'You can't do that!' She gasped. 'Too many people know there's something going on. Why do you think we were looking in the passages?'

'If you're thinking about your father then forget him. We caught him the minute he walked through the secret entrance.'

'What have you done with him?'

'He's safe enough until we start the fire that's going to break out in the house during the night. Owen's got it all worked out.'

'And Sarah Cameron? What about her? She saw you hiding in the derelict cottage. You'd better stop this before you go too far, George! You can't kill everyone. Sarah isn't here so how are you going to deal with her?'

He muttered something at her words and paused in midstride, his face shadowed in the reflected glare from his torch, making him look terrifying.

'I told Owen too many people knew what was going on,' he mused.

'Then stop now, before any real harm has been done,' she urged.

'It's out of my hands,' he muttered. 'Come on. We're working to a time table and mustn't fall behind.'

Jill swung her torch without thinking and crashed it against George's head. Half catching the swift movement, he tried to duck out of the way but the heavy weight slammed against his left temple and he gasped, losing his balance, falling to the ground.

Jill switched on her torch but the impact with George's head must have broken the bulb. She dropped it and snatched up George's torch, which lay on the ground, throwing a bright beam ahead.

She turned the light on George to see that he was trying to get up, groaning softly, a hand to his temple with a smear of blood showing between his fingers.

But suddenly his free hand shot out and grabbed Jill's ankle, and when he exerted his strength she stumbled forward and fell on top of him. His powerful arms encircled her and he snatched the torch from her frozen fingers.

'I don't want to have to hurt you,' he growled furiously. 'On your feet and don't give me any more trouble!'

Jill was dragged upright and they continued along the passage. Her sprained ankle was hurting again with little darts of pain stabbing through the joint. She was covered in dust and felt dishevelled, and she could feel her heart pounding loudly. Her fear had now been replaced with an unreal feeling that she was caught up in a bad dream. She clenched her teeth as George half-dragged her along the passage, able only to think about Robert and her father.

The passage began to widen and soon Jill saw they were approaching a rocky chamber. George was swinging the beam of his torch from side to side and she was able to make out the dimensions of the room, which was quite large. A gasp escaped her when she saw a figure stretched out on the stone floor just ahead. She hurried forward, but George pulled her back to his side, laughing quietly.

'It's Robert Cameron,' he said. 'He's going to learn that it doesn't pay to pry into other people's business!'

Jill saw that it was Robert lying on the ground, apparently unconscious.

'I want to see him!' she cried, struggling to break free from George's grasp.

'Stop it, you little fool!' George struck her across the face with the back of a powerful hand, and Jill staggered, dazed by the power of the blow.

The next moment a hand grasped her shoulder and spun her away from George, and she glimpsed Robert's figure looming beside her. George cried out as Robert's fist took him on the jaw, and he released his hold on Jill's wrist. The torch fell from George's grasp, and she dived for it, desperation driving all thoughts from her mind.

She managed to grab the torch as it rolled in the dust, and then Robert and George staggered over her and she was trapped on the hard ground.

The two men were struggling furiously, and Jill pushed herself to her feet when they rolled away from her. Turning the beam of the torch upon them, she saw Robert was getting the better of George, and suddenly George slumped to the ground and Robert straightened, breathing heavily, his face pale in the glare from the torch.

'Robert!' Jill gasped. 'We have to get out of here before Owen shows up.'

'Let him!' Robert was filled with fury. 'I have something to settle with him from years ago!'

'We have to call the police, Robert! George said they've got my father, too. We have to get him before they start this fire.'

'There won't be a fire!' Robert came to her side, put an arm around her shoulder and took the torch from her fingers. 'Let's get you out of here. You can phone the police while I look for your father. Owen has a lot to answer for. I was waiting for you to return with a torch when I heard a noise inside the cavity, and, as I turned, something hit me on the head.'

'George said Owen brought you in here.'

Jill explained what had happened when she got back to the bedroom.

'And you hit him with the torch!' Robert chuckled hoarsely. He turned the beam towards George and they saw he was beginning to stir. 'We must get you out of here! Come on. I have to find something to defend myself with.'

'I wonder where Owen is?' Jill said. 'He left you here, and didn't come back my way, so he must have gone along that passage over there.'

'And what about your father?' Robert demanded. His voice was low, and angry. 'I have to get your father out!'

'We can't split up,' Jill decided. 'There's only one torch between us, and it's far too dark to see without one so let's get out of here before Owen shows up again.'

'I think we're already too late,' Robert said harshly. 'There's a light coming towards us.' He grasped Jill's shoulder and pushed her against a wall, holding her close as he switched off the torch.

They stood in the darkness. Jill's heart was thudding and blood was hammering in her temples as silence closed in about them, enveloping them like a blanket.

She saw a tiny shaft of light glinting in the darkness ahead and closed her eyes, fighting to keep calm in the nightmarish situation. But fear for her father's safety was more important than her own fears and she drew a deep breath as the approaching light came ever closer.

Robert moved slightly and his lips touched her cheek.

'Whatever happens, don't move from this spot, Jill, so I'll know where you are in the darkness,' he whispered.

She could not reply. Her throat was tight with fear. The approaching torch-light became brighter. Robert whispered again, his voice just a faint hiss.

'Take the torch and switch it on when I tell you,' he commanded.

Jill felt his hand seeking hers, and she grasped the torch. Her fingers seemed stiff and awkward, but she felt for the switch and pressed her thumb against it until she felt it move slowly. Then she waited silently.

The approaching light drew still

nearer, and, to Jill's narrowed gaze, seemed to be almost on top of them. Then Robert shouted and she switched on the torch, throwing a brilliant shaft of light upon the ominous figure of Owen Craig, who paused, mouth open in shock, the torch in his right hand throwing its narrow beam at the ground.

Robert hurled himself forward as Owen was illuminated and Jill saw his right arm swing, hearing the crack of his knuckles smacking against Owen's jaw. Owen staggered, sagging almost to the ground, then recovered from his shock and kicked out at Robert, who was lunging at him. Watching both men fall, Jill kept the beam of her torch upon them as they struggled furiously.

Again Robert swung his fist, and then suddenly Jill was distracted by a noise at her back. She turned, swinging the torch away from Robert, and a gasp escaped her when she saw George running towards her, an oil lamp in one hand.

'The police are coming, Owen!' he shouted. 'Let's get out of here!' He couldn't see anything beyond the brilliance of Jill's torch and lifted a hand to shield his eyes. 'Get that light away from me,' he commanded. 'Owen, we're finished here. We'll have to make a run for it.'

Jill could see two lights at George's back, wavering slightly as whoever was carrying them came along the passage at a great pace.

'You're too late, George!' Jill screamed. 'Robert has got Owen.' She could hear Robert calling to her to give him some light and she flicked the beam towards him, to see Owen lying unconscious and Robert getting slowly to his feet, satisfaction showing in every dusty line of his face. He was even smiling a little, Jill noted with surprise as he stumbled past her to reach out for George, who had stopped uncertainly.

Just then two policemen arrived, waving torches.

'What's going on here?' one of them demanded.

Suddenly they were all bathed in bright but wavering torch-light. Jill narrowed her eyes against the yellow glare, feeling completely out of her depth.

'Robert Cameron!' one of the policemen said. 'We want Owen and George Craig!' He stepped forward quickly and seized George.

Jill caught the glint of handcuffs, and heaved a sigh of relief as they were snapped around George's thick wrists.

'Owen is lying over there,' Robert said, and the second policeman went to where Owen was stirring uneasily on the ground and quickly cuffed him.

'We received a telephone call from a Mr Telford informing us of the situation here,' one of the policemen reported. 'Your housekeeper showed us to a bedroom where a sliding panel had opened to reveal what the butler called a secret passage. Where is Mr Telford, does anyone know?'

'I'm right here!' Jill's father called from the darkness, and she turned swiftly to see a cone of torchlight coming towards them. Then her father's familiar figure materialised and Jill hurled herself towards him, tears of relief spilling down her cheeks as he put a protective arm around her shaking shoulders.

'Is there anyone else down here?' the policeman demanded.

'No, everyone is now accounted for,' Jim said. 'You've got your handcuffs on the right people. If we go back that way we'll come out in the library. Then we can make statements and tell you exactly what's been going on here.'

Jill felt weak at the knees as the policemen escorted Owen and George back along the passage, and she dropped back to Robert's side, putting the torch beam on him to check that he was not seriously hurt.

'I'm all right, Jill,' he said, smiling grimly. 'I've waited a long time to settle my differences with Owen, but I have to admit I didn't think I'd be doing it in such strange circumstances. And thanks for braving that passage on your own. You really helped me in there.'

'We all played our part — especially you, Dad!' Jill said, breathing deeply and wondering if her pulses would ever settle back to normal.

'You've got Robert to thank for telling me his suspicions,' her father replied.

He stepped into her bedroom and turned to take her hand. Jill heaved a sigh as she left the passage, and turned to Robert.

'Would you close the panel, Robert?' she said, and he did.

The policemen were escorting Owen and George from the room, and Alec was standing by the door, his face expressing deep concern.

'I'm glad that's over,' Jim said. 'I walked into trouble the instant I entered the secret entrance. Someone hit me over the head, and when I came to I was lying in a small chamber without a door. But I managed to find its secret panel.

'I went back out the way I came in and knocked at the front door. Alec let me in, and told me you had borrowed a torch from him so I guessed where you had gone. While Alec went to your room to check on you, Jill, I called the police.

'Then Alec said the panel in your room was open and there was no sign of you, so I left him to wait for the police and went back to the secret entrance in case anyone should try to escape through it.'

Jill clutched Robert's hand, and he gently squeezed her fingers.

'What are we going to tell Grandfather about Owen and George?' she said. 'The shock might kill him.'

'Don't worry about that,' her father replied. 'I'll try to break it to him gently. Let's just be grateful it's all over.'

Jill met Robert's gaze, and saw the love in his eyes, feeling the pressure of his hand on hers. Time would ease the pain of this horror, she knew, and then they would be free to enjoy the promise that beckoned. Knowing as she did that her life would never be normal again, it no longer held the fear it once had — the day she had entered Crag House . . .

THE END

We do hope that you have enjoyed reading this large print book.

Did you know that all of our titles are available for purchase?

We publish a wide range of high quality large print books including:
Romances, Mysteries, Classics
General Fiction
Non Fiction and Westerns

Special interest titles available in large print are:
The Little Oxford Dictionary
Music Book, Song Book
Hymn Book, Service Book

Also available from us courtesy of Oxford University Press:
Young Readers' Dictionary
(large print edition)
Young Readers' Thesaurus
(large print edition)

For further information or a free brochure, please contact us at:
Ulverscroft Large Print Books Ltd.,
The Green, Bradgate Road, Anstey,
Leicester, LE7 7FU, England.
Tel: (00 44) 0116 236 4325
Fax: (00 44) 0116 234 0205

AN UNEXPECTED ENCOUNTER

Fenella Miller

Miss Victoria Marsh has an unexpected encounter in the church with a handsome, but disagreeable, soldier who is recuperating from a grievous leg injury. Major Toby Highcliff believes himself to be a useless cripple, but meeting Victoria changes everything. Will he be able to keep her safe from the evil that stalks the neighbourhood and convince her he is the ideal man for her?

ANOTHER CHANCE

Rena George

School teacher Rowan Fairlie's life is set to change when Clett Drummond and his two young daughters take on the tenancy of Ballinbrae Farm. Clett insists he's come to the Highlands to help the girls recover from their mother's death, but Rowan suspects there's more to it. And why does her growing friendship with the family so infuriate the new laird, Simon Fraser? Is it simple jealousy — or are the two men linked by some terrible mystery from the past?

REBELLIOUS HEARTS

Susan Udy

Journalist Alice Jordan can't believe her misfortune when she literally bumps into entrepreneur Dominic Falconer. She is running a newspaper campaign to prevent him from destroying an ancient wood in his apparently never-ending pursuit of profit. However, when it becomes clear that local opinion is firmly on his side, Alice decides to go it alone. Someone has to stop him and she is more than ready for the battle. The trouble is — so is Dominic.

PASSAGE OF TIME

Janet Thomas

When charismatic Josh Stephens literally blows into her life, Melanie Treloar finds him a disturbing presence in the hostel she runs in west Cornwall. During his job of assessing some old mining remains Josh discovers a sea cave that holds an intriguing secret. When he is caught in a cliff fall — saving Melanie's niece — it is Melanie who comes to his rescue. Although this puts their relationship on a new level, can they solve the many problems that still remain?

ISLE OF INTRIGUE

Phyllis Mallett

Selina has come to Tarango to take up her inheritance — her father's sugar plantation — and she falls in love with the place from the moment of her arrival. There she meets the strikingly handsome Zack Halliday, who wants to buy her out, as does Hank Wayne, a tough American who won't take no for an answer. Then Fiona Stuart appears, wilful and jealous. Selina suspects the worst — and subsequent events prove her right . . .

VET IN POWER

Carol Wood

Despite the outrageous circumstances which bring Briony Beaumont to work for fellow veterinary surgeon Nick Lloyd, she is determined to make the best of it — and even she has to admit that Nick's surgery is impressive. But nothing else is certain with Nick . . . Briony is sure he is playing cat-and-mouse games with her emotions — so why can't she stop herself reacting to him?